This Journal belongs to:

. . . .

Gill Sims
WHY MUMMY DRINKS
The Journal

HarperCollins*Publishers*

About the Author

Gill Sims is the author of the hugely successful parenting blog and Facebook site 'Peter and Jane'. Her first book, *Why Mummy Drinks*, was the bestselling hardback fiction debut of 2017, spending over six months in the top ten of the *Sunday Times* Bestseller Charts, and was shortlisted for Debut Novel of the Year in the British Book Awards. Her second book, *Why Mummy Swears*, went straight to the top of the *Sunday Times* Bestseller Chart.

She lives in Scotland with her husband, two children and a recalcitrant Border Terrier who rules the house. Gill's interests include drinking wine, wasting time on social media, trying and failing to recapture her lost youth, and looking for the dog when he decides to go on one of his regular jaunts.

INTRODUCTION

Hello!

So, it's time for a New Year and a New You! Clean eating, yoga and meditation every morning at 5am and masses of mindfulness and self-care (does anyone else think the expression 'self-care' sounds rather like a millennial euphemism for interfering with oneself?). I'm only joking, obviously.

You're the proud owner of a journal called *Why Mummy Drinks*, so you almost certainly have no time at all for meditation, mindfulness or self-care (either of the self-help-book sort or the euphemistic sort), and your attempts at clean eating probably involve cramming down the children's rejected broccoli as well as their leftover chicken nuggets in between ferrying them to overpriced extracurricular activities. This journal isn't about promising to make you a better person, or a happier one, or a thinner one or even a wiser one, because there's nothing wrong with the person you are. What it hopefully will do, though, is give you somewhere that you can, for five minutes a day (or a week, it's not a school project, no one will deduct marks if you don't fill it in every day), record some of your memories of the year (good ones and bad ones, such as the magical moment your precious moppet rode a bike by themselves for the first time, or the equally magical moment you realised you had become such a dab hand with a packet of steri-strips that you could patch them up without recourse to spending four hours sitting in A&E when they fell off said bike doing something stupid that you TOLD them not to do BECAUSE THEY WOULD HURT THEMSELVES!).

As women and mothers, we are so busy looking after everyone else and ensuring they are **#makinghappymemories** that we can forget to remember our own lives and achievements, focusing only on those of our kids – and that is a bit pants really, because our lives and feelings and memories deserve to be recorded and remembered, too.

Or, you know, you can just skip straight to the drink recommendations at the end of each month and use the other pages to scrawl emergency notes to the school/draw rude pictures/leave passive-aggressive messages for your partner. Totally up to you.

Love Ellen xxx

Wishes for the year

The Year of #NailingIt

1. ....

2. ....

3. ....

4. ....

5. ....

6. ....

7. ....

8. ....

9. ....

10. ....

Wishes for the year

#NotFailingIt

1. ....

2. ....

3. ....

4. ....

5. ....

6. ....

7. ....

8. ....

9. ....

10. ....

JANUARY

January always starts with lists of those Important Resolutions.

Generally made under the influence of strong drink, they seem an excellent idea at 11.59pm on 31st December, when you are absolutely, DEFINITELY gonna learn French and you know wha', I'll learn Italian too, s'easy, prolly, an' then, an' then I'll chuck in my job an' go an' work for the UN! Wha' as? As translator obvioushly! An' I'll lose three stone. An' go Paleo, an' teetotal. Filthy booze, yuck! Nooooo! Not NOW! T'morrow! T'morrow is anuvver day! Yes! Scarlett O'Hara said so. NOW, I'm gonna have a tequila slammer an' a vol au vent. Mmmm, vol au vents so shmall! Look, I can get sixsh in my mouth at once!

And then you wake up to the cold, grey dawn of a January morning (why, why are January mornings so depressing? It doesn't matter how grey it was on the December morning you woke up to 24 hours earlier, it still wasn't as grim as a January morning), in dire need of a bacon sandwich and probably a Bloody Mary, and with the vague recollection of making a lot of rash promises last night that you hopefully haven't posted on social media, but, oh FML, yes you have, and lots of your so-called friends have commented below in French and Italian just to show off, even though they probably used Google Translate to do it, and none of those things you were going to last night seem like such a good idea any more.

So this January, instead of setting unachievable goals for things you are never going to do, why not focus on removing a few small things from your life that don't make you happy? For example, if you hate ironing (yes, this is very much my personal example, I hate ironing desperately, more than almost any other household chore) then reduce it to a bare minimum. Only iron work clothes, and school uniform on school photo days. Bin off ironing socks and pants and towels and t-shirts – if you have a partner who likes that stuff ironed, they can do it themselves, and your darling cherubs are only going to take your lovingly ironed stuff and chuck it under their bed for a week until it smells musty and then put it back in the wash while complaining that they have no pants.

Or maybe you don't mind chores but you are constrained by 'rules' that have nothing to do with modern life. My grandmother, as part of a lengthy list of things that were 'common' and must NEVER be done, used to insist that you could never wear orange and pink together ('clashing') or navy and black ('people will think you can't afford another pair of shoes'). So I spent years not wearing those colours together, and casting envious glances at people looking fabulous in orange and pink, or navy and black, and so I got a bit braver and cast Granny's 'wisdom' aside and felt rather daring (and a lot more stylish).

Or it could be something that makes you kinder to yourself, like stopping weighing yourself every day. Whatever it is, let this month be the month of Chuck It In The F*ck It Bucket, and give up one thing a week that isn't adding anything good to your life.

January 1st

What will be the first thing you Chuck in the F*ck It Bucket?

....

....

....

....

....

January 2nd

....

....

....

....

....

January 3rd

It's cold. Every magazine has titles screaming about diets and detoxes and all that makes me want to do is eat biscuits. Sometimes I ponder how thin I would be if only biscuits didn't exist. But then, maybe if I found myself in a biscuitless world, I would just invent them anyway.

....

....

....

....

....

January 4th

....
....
....
....
....
....
....
....

January 5th

Sometimes I think about just making a recording of me on a loop shouting 'SHOES TEETH COAT BAG' for the mornings to save myself the trouble. Obviously no one would still pay any attention to it, but it would free up more time for me to wonder if I'll ever get to drink a hot cup of tea again.

....
....
....
....
....
....
....

Something to look forward to

Give yourself a little something to look forward to
each month. A posh coffee out, tickets to something
interesting, a drink with a friend, or perhaps
even a weekend away?

....

....

....

....

....

....

January 6th Epiphany

There is a marvellous tradition in some places in Ireland where Epiphany is celebrated by giving all the women a day off in recognition of the fact that they have just spent several weeks running round making sure everyone else has a magical time over the festive season. This needs to be adopted more widely!

....

....

....

....

....

....

....

....

January 7th

....

....

....

....

....

....

....

....

....

January 8th

What will be the next thing you are going to Chuck in the F*ck It Bucket?

....

....

....

....

....

January 9th

....

....

....

....

....

....

January 10th Peculiar People Day

Apparently, yes, this is a thing. Although we are all peculiar in some way to other people!

....

....

....

....

January 11th

January 12th

January 13th Sceptics Day/Make Your Dream Come True Day

Do you believe in dreams, or are you a sceptic? Ah, the blissful irony of them falling on the same day ...

January 14th

....

....

....

....

....

January 15th

Week three of Chucking things in the F*ck It Bucket. Are you enjoying more freedom, or are you feeling twitchy about things not being done 'right'?

....

....

....

....

....

....

January 16th

....

....

....

....

....

January 17th

....
....
....
....
....
....
....

January 18th Thesaurus Day

I love thesauruses. We used to comb through an old *Roget's Thesaurus* at lunchtime when I was at school (it was an all-girls school and we weren't allowed to go out at lunchtime for fear we would Meet Boys in Burger King – don't judge me) and come up with new and innovative insults. Maybe you could learn a new word today, to dazzle and amaze your children. Unless of course learning new words is something you have given up for January, in which case your vocabulary is probably big enough.

....
....
....
....
....
....
....

January 19th

....

....

....

....

....

....

....

....

....

....

January 20th

The best thing about January is the SALES! The worst thing about January is being too poor after Christmas to take full advantage. My husband Simon is fond of telling me that even bargains cost money, which is plainly ridiculous as EVERYONE knows that a bargain is all about how much money you SAVED on it, not how much it cost.

....

....

....

....

....

....

January 21st Hugging Day/Squirrel Appreciation Day

Go oooonnnn! Give someone an extra hug today. Maybe don't hug an actual squirrel, though, I'm pretty sure there are laws against that. I am not a big fan of this newfangled method of hugging people as a greeting, I am sure it is not hygienic. I did remark on this to Simon and he suggested that it was probably more hygienic to hug other people than it was to hug animals that lick their own unmentionable parts and eat abandoned kebabs in the street. I remain unconvinced, I'm pretty sure some of the boys I knew in my youth would have happily licked their own balls if they could have and they quite probably ate abandoned street kebabs when they were drunk enough, and now they are respectable lawyers and doctors, probably going round hugging people willy-nilly.

January 22nd

Week four – what is the Chuck It In The F*ck It Bucket item this week?

....

....

....

....

....

January 23rd

....

....

....

....

....

January 24th

If ironing is one of your Chuck It In The F*ck It Bucket items, I can confirm that running hair straighteners over shirt collars does make an excellent substitute (just wear a jumper over the rest – it's January after all). Top tip: don't do it while you're wearing the shirt, unless you want to spend the day explaining how you got that burn on your neck. Obviously I didn't find that out the hard way . . .

....

....

....

....

January 25th Burns Night

I once asked a friend why so many English people celebrate Burns Night, and he said it was because they had tried celebrating Coleridge Day, but a day devoted to smoking opium and shouting at strangers about albatrosses hadn't really caught on. Which seemed fair.

....

....

....

....

....

....

....

....

January 26th

....

....

....

....

....

....

....

....

....

January 27th

....

....

....

....

....

January 28th

....

....

....

....

....

January 29th

The last day to pick something to Chuck in the F*ck It Bucket.

....

....

....

....

....

January 30th

....

....

....

....

....

....

....

....

....

January 31st

Things people without dogs will never say: 'I thought we had talked about this ... I know I briefly left you in the house alone, but that's not an excuse to sniff my tits!'

....

....

....

....

....

....

....

....

....

....

Winning at Life
Moment of the Month

What was the standout memory for you from this month? It doesn't have to be something big, or something amazing, it could just be a triumph over a small adversity. But when you look back at January, what is the one thing that happened that will stay with you most?

....

....

....

....

....

....

....

Tipple of the Month

Malibu Bellini

As we are probably all trying to at least go some way to undoing the excesses of Christmas, January's tipple should really be a Skinny Bitch, which is vodka, soda water and fresh lime. It is actually quite nice, and very refreshing, and I believe the lowest-calorie drink you can get (without just drinking neat vodka, which, unless you particularly like neat vodka, seems a little desperate), but it is a bit too predictable and also too depressing. January calls for something a little more cheery and decadent. So, the Malibu Bellini it is! It is also very simple, and most delicious. Don't be put off by the Malibu in this; many people have shuddered at the thought and muttered of unpleasant memories of teenage excesses, but after just one sip they have declared it not at all like the illicit Malibu and Cokes bought with dubious fake IDs in their youth.

So, all you need is a shot of Malibu and some fizzy wine – Cava, Prosecco, etc. It's not worth wasting proper champagne on this, unless you have more money than sense. Put the Malibu in the bottom of a champagne flute, top up with fizzy wine, banish the memory of snogging unsuitable boys at bus stops, forget the January sleet lashing against the window, and pretend you are on a tropical beach somewhere!

FEBRUARY

I am not a massive fan of February.

It seems such an *unnecessary* month – it's not the clean slate of January, it doesn't have the sparkle and fun of December, but it's just as grey and dark and cold, and it just sort of sits there, getting in the way of spring. And as if that wasn't enough, you have the fun of Valentine's Day to contend with, when you either sulk at your partner for being unromantic while scrolling through social media and telling yourself that people who are really happy shouldn't need to post at length about how amazing their other halves are and how much they love them. Or you feel slightly sorry for yourself because you are single and have no secret admirers, even though, when you think about it, secret admirers who know where you live are a little bit stalkery.

Anyway, since February is fit for doing little more than staying inside and wearing your pyjamas and cosy socks as much possible (and I complain my husband is unromantic . . .), it is also a good opportunity to catch up on those books, films or TV series you have always wanted to read/watch. Don't worry, this is not going to be a diktat that you must read one improving book every week, as well as watching an arthouse film and a Swedish noir TV series, while taking notes on them all in order to improve your mind – it's just about taking some time to catch up on something you've always meant to do. If you like improving books, arthouse films and Swedish noir (like I pretend to), that's fabulous of course, but equally, if Jackie Collins, rom coms and *Say Yes to the Dress* are more your cup of tea (my actual tastes), then go for it. So let's christen February 'Broaden Your Mind' month'.

Or if you never get time alone to watch a film, make your precious moppets watch something of your choice with you – sometimes they even enjoy it. Though before I sound like a smug Perfect Parent, normally they complain when I say I'm going to pick a film, because 'You'll make us watch one of those stupid *old* films'. I almost disowned Peter and Jane at the end of *Casablanca*, when they looked disgusted and said 'What was that film even about?' and I sobbed '*Love*! It was about *love*, you soulless beasts!'

February 1st

Any plans for how you are going to Broaden Your Mind? Are you aiming to read a new book? An old book? Are films and boxsets more your thing?

....

....

....

....

....

February 2nd Hedgehog Day

We're all familiar with the snuffling little prickly ones, but sadly their numbers are declining. If you have a garden, there are lots of simple things you can do to help hedgehogs, though – such as making small holes in fences to allow them to travel between gardens, or leaving out food (tinned cat or dog food or crushed cat or dog biscuits are perfect, but never leave milk for hedgehogs). In hot weather leave water out in a shallow bowl, as finding accessible water in a heatwave is big problem for hedgehogs. Leave small 'wild areas' for them to nest in (perfect excuse to not weed in the corners – you're not lazy, you're hedgehog friendly). And please, don't use slug pellets, which are toxic to hedgehogs and other wildlife. Of course, the good news is that if you encourage hedgehogs into your garden you won't need slug pellets as they will do an effective and natural job of keeping down the slugs and snails.

....

....

....

....

....

February 3rd

....

....

....

....

....

....

February 4th

....

....

....

....

....

February 5th

....

....

....

....

....

February 6th

Alongside the cutesy cards, featuring terrifying teddies that all look like they are about to wet their furry pants, there are CREME EGGS in the supermarkets, and there have been for over a month! This is WRONG, Creme Eggs are for Easter, and it is NOT EASTER YET.

....

....

....

....

February 7th

....

....

....

....

February 8th

How is The Mind Broadening coming along, or are you still 'rediscovering classics'?

....

....

....

....

February 9th

When did teddies become a Valentines thing? Why is it a sign of your love to give a grown woman a stuffed toy? I mean, if teddies are your thing, that's great, but how many people over the age of eight are actually into teddies?

....

....

....

....

....

February 10th

....

....

....

....

....

February 11th

Does anyone else ever find themselves thinking 'When I am a grown-up . . .' and then realise with horror that you are ticking pretty much every box that counts as being 'grown-up'?

....

....

....

....

....

February 12th

February 13th

Something to look forward to

You could go for a Mind-broadening Thing To Look Forward To this month. Like the ballet. I went to the ballet once. I fell asleep and had a lovely nap. Apparently this is Not The Point of the ballet though. I went to an opera once too. It's quite hard to sleep through opera though, there is a lot of ~~screeching~~ singing. If you are a philistine like me, you could just treat yourself to a lovely box set about men with big swords whose shirts keep falling off. By which I mean an important historical drama OBVIOUSLY!

....

....

....

....

....

....

February 14th Valentine's Day

We all knew it was coming. I find the whole idea of the modern concept of 'romance' quite annoying – 'here's a big, overpriced bunch of massive clichés, darling, for you to take a photo of and post on social media, a gesture that means not only do you know that I love you, but so does Susan Elliott who you sat next to in Mrs Jenner's class when you were five, and who used to pick her nose and eat the bogeys, but is now an annoyingly gorgeous, willowy blonde with a fabulous job in New York. BUT THIS WILL SHOW HER!' Surely the little things are far more romantic – a cup of tea unasked for, a lie in when you have a hangover, an unexpected hug. In fairness, though, while these things may be more romantic, they are also FAR less Instagrammable!

....

....

....

....

....

....

February 15th

Is your Mind Broadened yet? Have you managed to read anything or watch anything yet, or are you still shouting 'OMG, I have just read the same sentence fifteen times, please stop asking me questions about effing sharks!'

....

....

....

....

....

....

February 16th

....

....

....

....

....

....

....

....

....

February 17th Random Acts of Kindness Day

It's true, you never know when someone's small act will touch your life, or
when your tiny kindness will make a big difference to someone. So do something
nice – smile at someone, tell someone you love their shoes, leave a book you
liked on a bus for someone else to enjoy. You don't have to do anything that
costs you money, or much time or effort, but do one little thing to pass on a
little kindness.

....

....

....

....

....

....

....

....

February 18th Drink Wine Day

Need we say more? Feel free to record how you marked the day, though, even if it's just with a drink ring on the page . . .

....

....

....

....

....

....

....

....

February 19th

....

....

....

....

....

....

.... #✿X☠!!

....

....

....

February 20th National Chip Week

What idiot said February wasn't a great month? She was a FOOL! Drink Wine Day, *and* National Chip Week in the same month, what more could you want? Here are some things you might not know about chips – and remember, if you have questions about chips, don't be embarrassed to ask . . .

- Everybody has a different appetite for chips – some people like chips several times a day, other people like chips once a week or maybe once a month. Some people don't ever like chips.
- There are lots of different ways to eat chips. You can eat chips standing up, you can eat chips lying down. It's OK to like eating chips in whatever way is good for you.
- Remember, too, that you can put on weight the very first time you eat chips, even if you eat them standing up.
- And finally, don't let people pressure you into eating chips. If you don't fancy chips, it's OK to say no. (FOOL!)

....

....

....

....

....

February 21st

Does your Mind grow ever Broader? Are you racing through Mallory Towers, *or are you bogged down in* War and Peace? *Do you feel entirely Intellectual, or are you bored out of your (now broader) mind?*

....

....

....

....

February 22nd Single Tasking Day

Yes, today you are supposed to apply yourself wholeheartedly to only one thing at a time and give it your all. Give it a go, and then after thirty seconds, as you put the shopping away while shouting times tables questions at offspring and flinging together some semblance of a nutritious meal in less than five minutes, you can laugh and laugh and laugh at such an incredibly stupid concept that was clearly created by an idiotic man.

....

....

....

....

February 23rd

As part of Broadening Your Mind, And Theirs, you may have tried taking small children to a museum, whereby inevitably, even though they can read perfectly well, they will just stand in front of exhibits and demand 'What's that?' as if you were some sort of walking, talking Google, with all the answers to the ancient world at your fingertips, instead of them just READING THE DESCRIPTION on the exhibit!

....

....

....

....

February 24th

....

....

....

February 25th

Things people without dogs will never say: 'It's OK, the scary noise that made you jump was just your own fart!'

....

....

....

....

....

February 26th

....

....

....

....

....

February 27th

....

....

....

....

....

Pancake Day

Hurrah, it's Pancake Day! Because nothing says Traditional Fun like your children covering the kitchen in eggs and flour and demanding to be allowed to get third-degree burns on a frying pan before eating themselves into a sugar frenzy in a meal almost totally devoid of nutritional content. By all means put some token fruit on the table for them to ignore as they ladle sugar or syrup onto their pancakes and remind yourself that eggs are a good source of protein, then take comfort that Pancake Day only happens once a year.

February 28th

So, is your Mind now most Splendidly Broad? Did you manage a whole book or boxset? Did you romp through the Tyrol with the Chalet School, or did you plough through lengthy descriptions of 19th-century Russian farming while wondering when exactly Anna Karenina was going to get off with Vronsky?

....

....

....

....

....

Winning at Life
Moment of the Month

Was it your precious moppets declaring that they found
Swedish film noir more thought-provoking than they had
expected and would in future be giving up Pokémon in
favour of European cinema? No? I thought not . . .

....

....

....

....

....

....

....

....

Tipple of the Month

Tequila Sunrise

In these dark months, it's important to keep your vitamin intake up. Orange juice has lots of vitamin D and vitamin C, and what better way to enjoy it than going a bit retro with a Tequila Sunrise? And if you buy a decent brand of grenadine that is made with real pomegranates, you are definitely getting antioxidants and everything too, so you are practically drinking your five-a-day. Once you have bunged in a few cherries and a pink 'brella or two to 'garnish' it, your drink will look so cheery that you can't help but smile, however miserable the day!

1 shot of tequila
(your definition of a 'shot' is up to you!)

Orange juice, to taste

1 tbsp grenadine

Ice

Cherries and pink 'brellas galore!

Pop the tequila in a tall glass with ice, top up with orange juice, carefully pour the grenadine in down the side of the glass so it sinks to the bottom and gives that 'sunrise' effect, then add as many cherries and cocktail umbrellas as your heart desires. Drink in hand, sit back and pretend you are in a bar somewhere in about 1989.

MARCH

Hindsight really is a most wonderful thing.

If Only I'd Known when I was sixteen and sighing over being a size 12 in a Miss Selfridge skirt and feeling fat because of it, that I would end up keeping that skirt for over twenty years (mainly out of stubbornness because my father tried to make me get rid of it so often, due to his conviction that it was inappropriately short, and I had 'forgotten the rest of it'). And that one day I would look at it in astonishment at a) ever being thin enough to fit into something so tiny, and b) how much sizing has changed. That size 12 skirt would probably be more like a size 6 today, which is plainly ridiculous. If Only I'd Known that there was no point in pretending to boys that you are totally into obscure Indie bands and French literature and simply saved a lot of time by admitting that I loved Rick Astley and Jilly Cooper, because boys who really like you won't actually care. If Only I'd Known that mixing vodka and Hooch (remember Hooch?) was an incredibly bad, not to mention messy, idea and I wish I had gone to see Johnny Cash play live. I wish I had been less careless with my possessions and not lost so many things I loved, and I wish I had realised that youth does not equate to immortality and spent more time with friends who went too soon. I wish I had got on the property ladder as soon as I left university, back when such things were affordable, and I wish I had spent my student loan on a beautiful bronze in an Edinburgh antique shop window instead of on Topshop clothes and getting smashed on cheap cider – though going back to my regret about losing stuff, I probably would no longer have it, but I still think about and covet it. I wish I had told a lot more people to eff off. A LOT more people.

So you've probably guessed where this is going for this month. What do you wish you had known? What do you regret doing, or not doing? Do you think telling your kids these things will make any difference, or are there some things you can only learn through your own experiences? I mean, my son didn't listen when I told him not to stick his fingers in plug sockets, so why do I think he will listen when I explain to him why jägerbombs are almost always a bad idea? Though as a wise man once said, 'if "ifs" and "ands" were pots and pans, there'd be no need for Ikea...'

March 1st St David's Day

What is the biggest 'If Only I'd Known' when you were young? I wish I had known that it's fine not to take life seriously, that actually, life is too short to take seriously. I also wish I had known that polo necks did not make me look soulful and intellectual, but instead made me look like a giant walking pair of tits.

It's St David's Day today – the Patron Saint of Wales. St David was a vegetarian who only drank water and apparently lived until he was over one hundred years old. He also liked to stand up to his neck in cold water reciting scripture. He sounds like he was fun at parties.

....

....

....

....

....

....

....

March 2nd

....

....

....

....

....

....

....

World Book Day – First Thursday in March

Oh yes. Every parent's FAVOURITE DAY OF THE YEAR! Supposedly World Book Day falls on the first Thursday in March. Not that that will be any help to you in remembering when it is, as your children's school will most likely choose to hold it on a different, completely random day, thus leading to hyperventilating horrors from you when everyone else is posting their WBD costumes on Instagram and you have to tear the house apart in a panic looking for the specific letter which mentions in very small print at the bottom that actually your school is celebrating WBD in June, just to mess with your mind after you've already had a snarling argument with your precious moppets about how they are not going dressed as their favourite footballer or cartoon character because THEY ARE NOT IN A BOOK, FFS!

March 3rd

....

....

....

....

....

....

March 4th

....

....

....

....

....

March 5th Absinthe Day

Just while we're on the subject of things we wish we would have known/regret . . .
Apart from the other, more obvious evils of absinthe, I regret drinking it while
wearing a white top, because it stains horrendously.

....

....

....

....

....

March 6th

....

....

....

March 7th

....

....

....

March 8th International Women's Day

What is your biggest regretful 'If Only I'd Known'? I regret listening to Simon's 'reasons why it's not a good time to get a dog' arguments for so long and should have realised that, for him, there was never going to be a good time, and so I should have just gone and got a dog anyway years ago. But If Only I'd done that, I might not have ended up with Judgy Dog, AND I can't imagine life without him, even if he is currently attempting to push my laptop on the floor and smash it so he gets my undivided attention.

International Women's Day is a day to celebrate women's achievements, as well as remembering that the fight for equality is not over yet, especially for many women in developing countries. It's also a day for angry men on the internet to complain about there not being an International Men's Day and sulk when they are told there is one, in November.

....

....

....

....

March 9th

Do you ever find yourself lying awake at stupid hours of the morning, your brain whirling, pondering, not burning questions about the future of humanity or the meaning of life, but things like 'Who played the husband in *Indecent Proposal?*' or 'Who did Chloe in *Home and Away* end up marrying?' You know – important stuff that it's totally worth lying awake at 3am for (and if you're interested, it was Woody Harrelson, and her baby daddy's brother, but then she died, because, *Home and Away*)

....

....

....

....

March 10th

....

....

....

....

March 11th

There should be a special place in hell reserved for people who insist on having loud conversations via speaker phone while on public transport – and public floggings for every time they say 'I'm on the train!'

....

....

....

....

Something to
look forward to

In keeping with the theme of the month you could
go totally retro with this, and book tickets to something
like Rewind Festival. I have been trying to persuade
someone to go to Rewind with me for years, but no
bugger will, possibly because I try to persuade them by
saying things like, 'but the ginger love god Rick Astley,
who I still plan to marry one day, will be there.'

....

....

....

....

.... !◑#☠♔✳⌇

....

....

March 12th Napping Day

Why don't children and babies appreciate the wonder of naps?! Don't they know that one day they will be grown up and have jobs and children and an afternoon nap will literally be the biggest luxury imaginable?

....
....
....
....
....

March 13th

....
....
....
....
....

March 14th

....
....
....
....
....
....

March 15th

What do you want your children to know that you didn't, so they don't grow up sighing 'If Only I'd Known'? I wish I had known how much of my adult life would be spent working out which bin should go out this week. I know, recycling is GOOD and we need to save the planet, and that's all great, BUT WHY IS IT SO EFFING COMPLICATED? It's JUST BINS! When did putting the bins out get so bloody difficult? I swear you need a PhD in Bin Management to actually know what goes out when! I thought I had sussed it by just waiting for a braver neighbour to put their bins out first and then following suit, but then an evil friend of mine says sometimes she puts the WRONG bin out on purpose, just to mess with her neighbours. What 'ifs' or 'ands' would you tell your children to look out for?

....

....

....

....

....

....

March 16th No Selfies Day

Will duckfacing one day be considered a seminal moment in a seismic cultural shift, or will people finally realise it just made them look like dicks, not ducks?

....

....

....

....

....

....

March 17th St Patrick's Day

The Patron Saint of Ireland, famous, of course, for driving the snakes out of Ireland and the only national Saints Day that anyone really properly celebrates, whether they are Irish or not. Why is this? Is it just that the Irish are much better at parties? Is it because other Saints Days are quite sombre occasions whereas this is just a massive knees-up and an excuse to get pissed? It's not even as if green is a particularly flattering colour on a lot of people ... Also, just FYI, St Patrick was probably actually Welsh.

....

....

....

....

....

....

March 18th

....

....

....

....

....

....

....

....

....

Spring Equinox

The Spring Equinox (somewhere between March 19 and 21, depending on the year), and the official First Day of Spring. Would it be madness to consider packing away the winter boots and perhaps daringly breaking out some flirty little shoes as part of a jaunty spring 'look'?

March 19th

....

....

....

....

....

....

....

....

March 20th

Have you ever found your 'parent life' spilling over into 'real life'? Like, barking at an innocent stranger to do up their shoelaces, before they FALL OVER AND HURT THEMSELVES!!!???

....

....

....

....

March 21st

....

....

....

March 22nd

Is there one moment in your life that changed your future? If Only I'd Known what was about to happen to utterly change my life ... The night I met my husband, if I hadn't arrived a few minutes early to meet a friend (and I am NEVER early for anything, something that drives Simon mad) or if my friend hadn't been a few minutes late (probably assuming that there was no point in arriving on time because I would be late), then he might never have started talking to me, and the entire course of both our lives could have been completely different. Our darling children, Peter and Jane might never have existed! All because of just a few minutes here or there ...

....

....

....

....

March 23rd

March 24th Earth Hour

You may well have to provide another costume for this, most likely in the brief moment between your precious moppet enquiring after the costume you had no idea was required and leaving for school that same morning.

Clocks Go Forward

Whose idea was this? Whose? Is there a single person who benefits from this? It's not the farmers, because they are not stupid enough to believe that fiddling with the clocks gives them 'extra' time. It's not the school children, because the Powers That Be could just pick the time that gives the best light for kids going to school/coming home. All it does is MESS WITH OUR MINDS as we try to explain to unsleepy children that it really IS bedtime!

March 25th

....

....

....

....

....

....

....

....

March 26th

....

....

....

....

....

March 27th

There should be a special internationally recognised sign that you can make for
when you really need a wee and have to go to a public loo, so that when you come
out looking extremely relieved, you can still make it clear that it was JUST A
WEE!

....

....

....

....

....

March 28th

....

....

....

....

....

March 29th

Is there anything to be learnt from thinking about the things you wish you had known/regretted/did/didn't do? Or is there frankly no use worrying about the 'If Only I'd Knowns', and we should just make the most of dodgy haircuts, terrible lovers and dubious cocktails?

....

....

....

....

....

March 30th

....

....

....

....

....

March 31st

Things people without dogs will never say: 'Hi, I'm looking for a sofa to buy in a nice shade of mud with hints of hair and tones of Bonio.'

....

....

....

....

....

Mother's Day

Traditionally, this is actually about returning home to your 'mother church'. Now that most of us are godless heathens, it has become a lovely day to supposedly celebrate your mother. What it mostly is, in fact, is a day for mothers across the land to bravely eat their way through a dubious breakfast in bed, while making enthusiastic noises about the mystery lumps of glitter their precious moppets have made at school as a 'surprise' and bestowed upon them, while scrolling though social media and trying to suppress the nagging doubt that everyone else has better children who love them more. They don't. They just have better filters.

Winning at Life
Moment of the Month

Did you ever think when you were younger how
much you would come to hate the words **#soblessed**?

....

....

....

....

....

....

....

....

Tipple of the Month

Pinot Noir

As we move into spring, why not try a lighter red? Some people describe Pinot Noir as the white wine of red wines (not, admittedly, wine buffs) but it is a little lighter for those spring evenings, when you're not quite ready to break out the pink sunshine wine but nor do you want one of those heavy winter reds. With top notes of eternal hope and optimism that this year your children might embrace your Famous Five fantasies and spend the summer on jolly japes and frolics, this pairs well with leftover fish fingers and is best enjoyed while hiding in the kitchen, lying that there is no tomato sauce left.

APRIL

So, hopefully, fingers crossed, touch wood, etc., we have made it through another winter and spring is finally here.

The daffodils should be blooming, the bluebells starting to come out and the trees budding and bursting into life. There might, just MIGHT be sunshine too. There are also two weeks of school holidays to get through, which however **#soblessed** you feel towards your precious moppets, and however much you enjoy them being off school, still represents two weeks of expense in the form of extra childcare, days off and days out to entertain them to create those all-important **#happymemories**.

But now that the weather is nicer, you can get outside more a little more. It's been a long winter, and I do sometimes genuinely worry about the dangers of rickets for my children – along with scurvy (I know, I seem to have some sort of obsession with obscure Victorian ailments). This year as part of **#ProjectAntiRickets**, we should take a bit of outdoor time for ourselves.

Most forays outside as parents centre around the children, while we simply trail in their wake like anxious donkeys, lugging panniers of snacks for their insatiable hunger and water bottles for them to ignore while they plead for Fruit Shoots and brandishing wet wipes at them in a desperate attempt to stave off salmonella/stop them eating dog poo. This year we should take a bit of outdoor time for ourselves, too, instead of it being all about trips to the park for the kids to tell us they are bored and there is nothing to do until it's time to come home, at which point they will be having the BEST TIME EVER and you are a terrible mother for making them leave.

If you have childcare, walk to the pub and meet a like-minded friend, although technically that probably isn't entirely in the spirit of getting outside more and reconnecting with nature. Although wine is made from grapes and grapes are a plant, so you know, you could argue it still counts . . .

Even if you don't get a chance to go outside by yourself, drag the little darlings on a walk by a canal or a river, or to a different park or a botanic garden. Most of these will be free, and will give the kids something else to complain about while they try to hurl themselves into the water/off a deathslide/through the greenhouse glass, while you shout 'LOOK AT THE MOTHER-EFFING NATURE! STOP FIGHTING! LOOK AT THE FLOWERS! Ummm, they're called flowers. YELLOW flowers' and resolve to Google plant names when you get home. It will give some sterling opportunity for smug social media photos of what a lovely time you are having. As long as you use a filter that hides the tears, and crop the blood out of shot.

April 1st April Fool's Day

Did anyone think your announcement that this month you would all be spending more time outside as part of your grand **#ProjectAntiRickets** was just a massive April Fool's joke?

....

....

....

....

....

April 2nd

....

....

....

....

April 3rd

WHERE ARE ALL THE SOCKS? Why is there always at least one odd sock in every single wash? Where do the other socks go?

....

....

....

....

....

April 4th Vitamin C/Carrot Day

Yes, there is A Day For Literally Everything. However, as part of getting outside more, you could encourage your children to plant some carrots today. You could even be really optimistic and kid yourself they will be more likely to eat carrots they have grown themselves. If you don't have a garden, you could get carrot tops to sprout in a saucer of water. If you're not a gardener, however, you could always just celebrate Vitamin C Day with a nice Kir Royale. Crème de Cassis is made with blackcurrants, which are very high in vitamin C!

....

....

....

....

April 5th

....

....

....

....

April 6th

....

....

....

....

Something to look forward to

If you are very much in favour of the Great Outdoors, obviously you could make this month's treat an outdoor one. On the other hand, if you are not enjoying the Outdoors theme this month so much, your treat could be staying inside, where it is warm and safe and there is no pollen or bitey things. Apart from children, obviously . . .

....

....

....

....

....

....

....

....

April 7th

There is no sleep so deep, so sweet, so profound, nor so bitter to be wrenched from as those stolen minutes when you accidentally hit 'off' instead of 'snooze', only to wake with a hideous jerk and the realisation that your whole day is banjaxed now and you will never catch up on the lost time EVER!

....

....

....

....

April 8th

Have you managed to spend any time outside on your own as part of
#ProjectAntiRickets?

....

....

....

....

....

April 9th

....

....

....

....

....

April 10th

April 11th Pet Day

Frankly, what better day to spend some time outside with your pet? Weather permitting, obviously, as rabbits and guinea pigs will not thank you for being dragged out of a warm hutch into a hurricane, and cats will just plot to kill you if you attempt such a thing. Actually, cats will just plot to kill you, full stop.

April 12th

April 13th

Something they don't tell you when you have a baby: having a cold is never quite the same again, as every cough and sneeze plays a game of Russian Roulette with your pelvic floor ...

....

....

....

....

April 14th

....

....

....

....

April 15th

Are your kids now adorable Famous Five-style moppets, tumbling about with rosy-cheeked abandon, or do they huddle hollow-eyed and shell-shocked beneath a bush, hiding from the vicious bright glare of the sun, begging to be reunited with their electronics, and for the hideous experiment that is #ProjectAntiRickets to be abandoned before they report you to Childline?

....

....

....

....

April 16th

....

....

....

....

....

April 17th

....

....

....

....

....

April 18th World Heritage Day

The perfect excuse to drag grumbling children to local sights of important historic and cultural interest, while they either tell you they are 'bored' and you shout 'only boring people get bored' or they attempt to climb on the ancient and venerable monuments and damage them so you have to leave hastily.

....

....

....

....

....

April 19th

April 20th

There are few things as shameful as testing your child on their multiplication tables and then having an argument with them about how 8 × 7 is 64, only for it to turn out that they were right, and it is in fact 56. Oh the humanity!

Easter

Easter is now mainly about chocolate, bunnies and the
Daily Mail getting enraged about spurious claims that
political correctness is going to ban Easter eggs. But it can
also be about family and fun and painting eggs and making
new traditions. Or you could just go to Ikea.
Like 99% of the rest of the country.

April 21st

*Are you enjoying **#ProjectAntiRickets**, or do you want to retreat to a cave far from people and nature, with a family-size pack of Kettle Chips and the* EastEnders *omnibus?*

....

....

....

....

....

....

....

....

April 22nd

....

....

....

....

....

....

....

....

....

April 23rd St George's Day

The Patron Saint of England. Sadly, apparently the stories about him slaying a dragon are a metaphor for the devil. All the best stories turn out to be metaphors. Fun fact: William Shakespeare, who was partly responsible for immortalising St George in English tradition with Henry V's battle cry at Agincourt of 'Cry God for Harry, England and St George', is believed to have been born and died on St George's Day.

....
....
....
....
....

April 24th

....
....
....
....

April 25th

Manflu vs childbirth. Which is more painful. Discuss . . .

....
....
....
....

April 26th Take Your Sons and Daughters to Work Day

Proof that there are no limits to the stupidity of humanity. It will surely culminate in what is tactfully referred to as a 'career-limiting event'.

....

....

....

....

....

April 27th

....

....

....

....

....

April 28th

....

....

....

....

....

April 29th

*Are you glad that **#ProjectAntiRickets** is over and are you now planning on spending the rest of the year under a duvet, or are you converted to the Great Outdoors?*

....

....

....

....

....

....

....

....

April 30th

Things people without dogs will never say: 'How many times have I told you not to drink out of the toilet?'

....

....

....

....

....

....

....

Winning at Life
Moment of the Month

Was it an outdoors winning at life moment? Curiously,
many of my most **#FML** moments seem to take place outdoors.
Almost always in the presence of multiple witnesses.

....

....

....

....

....

....

....

....

Tipple of the Month

Pimm's

Since it's all been about getting outside, it's got to be the most outdoorsy drink in the world, that was just made to be sipped on verdant lawns, in cottage gardens, beside tennis courts and cricket pitches and on village greens. Or failing that, in any outdoor space you can muster that doesn't contain trampolines, rusting scooters and swingball sets, while you listen to your neighbours arguing about why he never brings the bloody washing in. It is frankly not worth making a glass of Pimm's, it should be served by the jug, even when you are alone – just add more lemonade.

Add whatever fruit takes your fancy – strawberries are good, but apples and cucumber are also traditional. Raspberries tend to go soggy and leave bits in your teeth, but whatever floats your boat. Maybe not kiwi fruit, that might be weird. Or mango or anything too exotic, unless you are stuck and fancy experimenting – sometimes that is where the best concoctions come from, like the night my friend Hannah and I discovered that gin and orange squash is actually rather nice.

Fruit

Mint

Pimm's No 1

Gin/vodka (optional)

Lemonade or soda water

Ice

Chop all your fruit and tear your mint leaves and pop them into the jug with some ice, then pour in a good slug of Pimm's – if you are going for the turbo-charged version, add a generous dash of vodka or gin and top up with lemonade to taste. If you find lemonade too sweet, use soda water, though it can be a bit cough-syrupy.

Don your shady hat and recline and quaff while thinking jolly Famous Five-ish thoughts.

NB, the fruit ends up somewhat alcoholic, so do not let your little darlings eat it, as this is a) a terrible waste, and b) frowned upon when they are somewhat dazed and confused afterwards.

MAY

May always feels like the point when the year has definitely turned.

Everything is green, blossoming and flowering, those grey, bare, despondent winter days seem far behind us, and the world is bright and hopeful again (well, it should be anyway, you can never be 100% sure in the British Isles, of course, as there is always the possibility of going through all four seasons in one day. But yet we remain optimistic).

So, with the start of the summer upon us (potentially), why not try Venturing Into The Unknown with some new things this month as well? In theory, having ditched some things you hate doing in January, you might even have some extra time (if you're not frantically using it reading and watching films outside while thinking about the things you didn't know in your lost youth and filling in a journal that seemed like a good idea at the time), so you could use that to start doing something new.

It can be something big, like joining a class to learn a new skill. Do you remember when people used to write into problem pages, asking how to meet a man, and they were always told to join a class in 'car maintenance' or something? Has anyone, in the history of the world *ever* actually met a man at a car-maintenance class? No man I have ever met in my life would go to a car-maintenance class, because that would imply that there are things about cars that he doesn't know. Or you can try something small, like starting a jigsaw puzzle because you always loved them as a kid and haven't done one in years. You could go skinny dipping in an icy loch; you could start going to the library with your kids once a week; you could take up meditation (every time I have tried to meditate, I end up thinking about what I can eat when I am finished, it is a terrible thing to have one's inner peace so trampled by one's inner greed); you could teach yourself to rebuild your oven via YouTube videos; you could start a family games night (if you're brave); you could take up base jumping, or knitting, or start a blog or write a book!

May 1st May Day

What is going to be the first Venture Into The Unknown that you are going to try? According to Jilly Cooper, May 1st is also traditionally the day to start taking one's marital unpleasantnesses outside. Which would certainly be a New and Unknown Venture for many of us, though I suspect most of the Unknowns would involve foreign objects creeping into your pants at unexpected moments . . .

....
....
....
....

May 2nd

....
....
....

May 3rd

I wonder how much time we waste in a year that could be spent on fun things, or at least useful things, just deleting emails from Nigerian generals and their friends, promising us millions, or true love, or at the very least dubious rebates from Amazon or the taxman.

....
....
....
....

May 4th No Pants Day

Although I think this is actually an American day, and what they mean is 'no trousers', I think the British translation is much funnier, and would certainly be something different when you are embracing new things. Unless it's not a new thing for you. In which case, no one is judging you. Much.

....

....

....

....

....

May 5th

....

....

....

....

....

May 6th

....

....

....

....

....

Something to look forward to

A new thing? Or stay in your comfort zone, because your pelvic floor is not what it was, and there is only so much excitement it can cope with in a month?

....

....

....

....

....

....

May 7th

....

....

....

....

....

May 8th

How are you enjoying the Unknown Ventures?

....

....

....

....

May 9th

Is there any feeling in the world that can quite match that fleeting blissful moment when you take your bra off, and just for a second it feels like every hope and dream you have ever had has just come true. Until you realise when they reach the floor, that it is actually very cold even for May.

....

....

....

....

....

May 10th Stay Up All Night Night

Ah ha ha ha ha. Like that is a challenge to a parent! And it certainly won't fall under the heading of 'trying something new'. Do you remember when we used to stay up all night for *fun*? Dancing or talking or drinking – or all three. What a bloody stupid idea! Why did no one tell our foolish youthful selves 'Go to bed, you bright young things, go now, go to your empty beds, with no small people trying to climb in and kick you, go, RIGHT NOW, and sleep for hours and hours, with no one to poke you in the eye to ask who your favourite Pokémon is, slumber uninterrupted, safe in the knowledge that you will not have to hurtle out of bed at a rate of knots to break up WW3 because he LOOKED AT HER. Sleep and ENJOY it and stockpile every little snatch of shuteye you can possibly get, because one day, you will be parents and sleep will be but a distant memory for many many years. And it is years, not months, because after your baby starts sleeping through, they become a toddler and they have bad dreams, and they have no concept of time so they get up at 3am like that is a normal thing. And then they become small children who in theory can tell the time, and you know they can because you spent eleventy bloody billion hours doing 'Telling The Time' worksheets with them for their homework and yet they still think that sparrow's fart is a decent hour to wake you up to ask if you think a badger monkey or a gorilla donkey would win in a fight, however many times you tell them that *it is 5am and you don't give a proverbial's who would win in a totally hypothetical fight and if they dare utter the words 'but just SAY if they DID exist and had a fight' you will not be responsible for your actions.* How I wish I had known the precious value of sleep in the days before children!

....

....

....

....

....

....

May 11th

....
....
....
....
....

May 12th

When did kale become a thing? When? Why? Even Judgy Dog won't eat it, he was appalled the day I put some in his dinner and picked it all out! It is only palatable if smothered in oil and salt and other unhealthy things, yet it is marketed as a health food. I think it is all a cunning conspiracy by the kale farmers . . .

....
....
....
....
....

May 13th

....
....
....
....
....

May 14th

....

....

....

....

....

May 15th

*Have you tried a few different Unknowns, or have you picked one new thing
to get to grips with?*

....

....

....

....

....

May 16th

....

....

....

....

....

May 17th World Baking Day

Because we don't have enough to do. And helpfully, schools like to tell children about days like this, possibly in revenge for teachers spending their days in fetid classrooms stinking of child farts and half-chewed crayons, and trying to wrangle overexcited children who are losing their minds with excitement at the prospect of a krispy cake at the school bake sales.

....

....

....

....

....

May 18th

....

....

....

....

....

May 19th

....

....

....

....

....

May 20th

Have you ever ignored the laundry for ONE DAY and then found that somehow it is threatening to take over your house, and you are slightly scared you might die in a dirty-laundry-related avalanche? Apparently there are people out there who only do laundry once a week – how do they manage this?

....

....

....

....

May 21st

....

....

....

....

....

May 22nd

Now you have had a few Ventures Into The Unknown, and tried some new things, which are now hopefully no longer Unknown, have you kept any of them up?

....

....

....

....

....

May 23rd

....

....

....

....

....

May 24th

....

....

....

....

May 25th Tap Dance Day

I took tap-dancing classes a few years ago, when I was trying to break out of
a rut and try new things. I was convinced it would be my hidden talent, and
I would be a tap-dancing star. I bought pink sparkly leg warmers and silver tap
shoes in anticipation of unleashing my dazzling skills upon the world. I was so
bad at tap-dancing. I mastered a few basic steps, but when they tried to make
me do hands and feet together, I fell over. People saw. So I am still trying to
discover my hidden talent.

....

....

....

....

May 26th

....
....
....
....
....

May 27th

Do you ever look at Amazon or Facebook's 'Things You Might Also Like' suggestions and think 'WTF? What in my browsing history has led you to believe that I might ever be interested in this?' And then worry about what opinions they have formed of you, that they think this is where your true interests actually lie . . .?

....
....
....
....
....

May 28th

....
....
....
....
....

May 29th

Has going out of your comfort zone to Venture Into The Unknown given you back more of a sense of who you are? Or would you just like me to stop with the Self-help W*nk and get on with the Tipple of the Month?

....

....

....

....

....

May 30th

....

....

....

....

....

May 31st

....

....

....

....

....

....

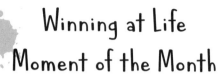

Winning at Life
Moment of the Month

Did you, after all, discover your **#hiddentalent**?
I am still searching for mine. Along with my dignity.

....

....

....

....

....

....

....

....

Tipple of the Month

Pinot Grigio Blush

As it is practically summer, it is definitely time to break out the Pink Sunshine Wine! I've picked a Pinot Grigio Blush, because it's what I like, but there are Pink Sunshine Wines for all palates, from very sweet to bone dry. Rosé wine is generally characterised by top notes of telling the kids they are either in or they are out, and to make up their minds, with hints of last year's sunscreen, which is probably still fine. Best enjoyed while breaking up fights over whose turn it is to go on the trampoline, and browsing unaffordable luxury villas on the Algarve.

JUNE

When summer starts in earnest, music starts to seep out into the atmosphere.

The muffled crackle of your neighbour's radio from an adjoining garden, the thudding base booming out of a boy-racer's ridiculously over-modified hatchback, with a stereo that's worth more than its engine, the sound of a forgotten song drifting out of an open window. Wet Wet Wet's 'Love Is All Around' instantly transports me back to the summer of 1994, when I was sixteen and ended up having to go and see *Four Weddings and a Funeral* three times, because I had somehow ended up seeing three different boys and so had to go and see it with them all. (With hindsight, why didn't I just tell the second two I had already seen it with friends?) Pulp's 'Disco 2000' is both roaring along to the words while jumping up and down and necking vodka and coke in Edinburgh's sadly departed Subway nightclub, and also watching a poor girl stand up to make a speech at a very grand ball and starting by saying 'My name is Deborah . . .' only for the whole room to turn around and bellow 'IT NEVER SUITED YA!' (It did suit her, we were just all drunk and thought we were being clever.) And House of Pain's 'Jump Around' always reminds me of being fifteen, with about six of us crammed in my friend's Fiesta, the car shuddering as much from the vibrations of the stereo as from the overloading. So if 'Jump Around' comes on the radio while I am driving back from Waitrose in my husband's Sensible Grown-up Car, I am always a reckless and irresponsible teenager again, instead of a middle-aged mother of two.

Too much of the time music is background noise, or we end up listening to nursery rhyme CDs or singing *The Wheels on the Bus*, instead of *Wuthering Heights* (yes, I do know the dance as well as all the words, and yes, it is my party piece). This month, let's make it about the TUNES (I can feel my children cringing at me using the word 'Tunes' to describe music, but I WILL bring back the nineties single-handedly if it kills me) and actually *listen* to music that you love. And possibly, even go wild and crazy and discover some new music – although everyone sensible knows that Music ended at midnight on the 31 December 1999, and there has been no new music since, only hideous noise. But something out there might surprise us, amidst the horrid cacophony of Young People's Music.

June 1st

So let's get thinking about the TUNES for this month! What was the first album you ever bought?

....

....

....

....

....

June 2nd

....

....

....

....

....

June 3rd

....

....

....

....

....

Something to look forward to

Once upon a time, this could have been a new CD, or cassette tape, or even an LP. Treating yourself to a new download isn't quite the same, is it? On the other hand, at least in later life we won't have to endure the indignity of our offspring going through our download collection and scoffing at it, before stealing anything even slightly cool for themselves, like we did with our parents.

....

....

....

....

.... !◑#☠✻⚡〜

....

....

June 4th

June 5th Running Day

You either love running or you hate it. I hate it, but I still do it, because it's over fairly quickly and it burns enough calories to enable me to eat pies. The last time I went running, cows looked at me (actual cows, I'm not being rude about passers-by). It's discombobulating to be judged by cows. The only thing that makes running bearable is LOUD music. Though even the loudest music cannot entirely drown out the nagging fear about how ridiculous you must look that even the cows are appalled by you.

June 6th

Is there any joy that can compare with finding a forgotten packet of biscuits in the cupboard? A joy made all the more potent by the rarity of its occurrence, because let's face it, how often do any of us actually forget about biscuits?

....

....

....

....

....

June 7th

....

....

....

....

....

June 8th

Are there actually any new TUNES out there that aren't by Ed Sheeran?

....

....

....

....

....

Exams

Those of you with teenagers will now be in Exam Hell.
This largely consists of trying not to nag your darlings and
thus add to their stress while at the same time wanting to shake
them and shout 'FFS, THESE EXAMS ARE IMPORTANT,
ARE YOU ACTUALLY STUDYING OR ARE YOU
JUST SNAPCHATTING?! You cannot build a career out
of Snapchat Streaks, you know!' Your teenagers will probably
respond to your hovering solicitations and suggestions that a
BIT of revision wouldn't go astray by telling you to 'chill', 'back
off' or assuring you that it is all 'fine' while inhaling the
contents of your fridge and cupboards and rejecting your
proffered 'brain food' of fish and broccoli in favour
of a diet of Pringles and Doritos.

June 9th

⚡☇#✧!

....

....

....

....

....

....

June 10th

....

....

....

....

....

June 11th

Packed lunches should take no more than five minutes to make (unless you are carving Pokémon figures out of carrots – I have no idea why anyone would do that) so why are they so utterly annoying and soul-destroying to make?

....

....

....

....

....

June 12th

....
....
....
....
....
....

June 13th

....
....
....
....
....
....

June 14th World Blood Donor Day

Blood donors save lives every single day, sometimes more than one life in a day. What else can you do in an hour that can have such far-reaching results?

....
....
....
....
....

June 15th

Which song never fails to make you smile? Even if you are simultaneously shouting at the radio that there is NO WAY this TUNE can be a 'Golden Oldie' because it was only in the charts a few months ago?

....

....

....

....

....

....

....

Father's Day

What better way for all the daddies out there to celebrate their special day than by spending it in precious one-to-one time with their darling children? Best the mummies keep out of the way, and struggle bravely on by going and doing something lovely while the daddies enjoy their special bonding time. And for all the mums out there doing the dad's job too, you are amazing, and well done!

June 16th

It's JUNE! Therefore, the next person who posts a chirpy meme on social media, possibly involving Minions, about how many days it is till Christmas, I will FIND them, and I will HURT them!

....

....

....

....

....

....

....

....

June 17th

....

....

....

....

....

....

....

....

....

June 18th International Picnic Day

I love the idea of a picnic. Sadly, the glorious, shady-hatted, wicker-hampered, floral-blanketed vision in my head rarely coincides with the reality of shouting at children to please eat their sandwich because there is nothing wrong with it, while fending off wasps and eyeing the looming black clouds with dismay. But still I persist, convinced each time I pack the hamper (TK Maxx, very good value) that this time it will be a splendid day of japes with Peter and Jane while I recline elegantly on my blanket, and a soundtrack of laid-back jazz plays somewhere in the background. I am not entirely convinced that anyone manages the sort of picnics I dream about when they have children. It does seem to be an incessant round of breaking up fights, explaining why you can't just eat cake and looking in dismay at the strawberries smeared down your new linen skirt, rather than the stuff that **#happymemories** are made of. I am hopeful that the children will have **#happymemories** of our picnics though, even if I twitch and shudder at the memories. No doubt after enough time has passed, I will forget the near drownings, the vicious swans, the appalled French family who attempted to picnic next to us and swiftly moved away due to the noise and borderline violence resulting from my suggestion of a nice game of rounders, and I will only remember the good bits. There must be some, I'm sure.

....

....

....

....

....

....

....

....

....

....

....

June 19th

....

....

....

....

....

....

June 20th

....

....

....

....

June 21st Longest Day

There are two very popular ways to celebrate the Summer Solstice – one is by dancing naked round a bonfire, covered in woad, the other is by shouting 'I don't care if it's still light, just go to sleep FFS!' at your children.

June 22nd

What is your 'sad song'? Is it a good, depressing ballad to have a thorough wallow in your own misery to, or is it a bangin' upbeat TUNE that helps you pull yourself out of the Slough of Despond? Would you like me to stop shouting TUNE now? Have I turned into the embarrassing auntie at the family party trying to bust her twenty-year-old Ibiza moves on the dancefloor after one too many peach schnapps and lemonades?

....

....

....

....

....

June 23rd

....

....

....

June 24th

Few minutes tick by slower than those minutes when you are waiting for your toastie to toast. Judgy Dog agrees, he is very partial to a cheese toastie.

....

....

....

....

June 25th Global Beatles Day

Why not try answering all your precious moppets' inane questions today only using Beatles' lyrics or song titles? It's easier than you think!

....

....

....

....

June 26th

....

....

....

....

June 27th

Things people without dogs will never say: 'If you eat my socks, we can't go for a walk!'

....

....

....

....

....

June 28th

....
....
....
....
....
....

June 29th

Has listening to some different music, whether new or old, changed how you feel about music or how you listen to your TUNES? OK, I solemnly promise I will never say 'TUNES' again now.

....
....
....
....
....

June 30th

....
....
....
....
....
....

Winning at Life
Moment of the Month

If there was a soundtrack to your winning
moment this month, what would it be?

....

....

....

....

....

....

....

....

Tipple of the Month

Chardonnay

A perhaps controversial wine choice, but selected for this month because it reminds me of sunbathing on the roof outside my student flat in Edinburgh with music blaring and a bottle of Australian chardonnay from the Vicky Wines downstairs and thinking we were so terribly sophisticated. It was a dreadful shock to learn that chardonnay was considered rather déclassé, as in those days I wasn't really aware of any other white wines. There still seems to be a bit of snobbishness around chardonnay, but there are some really lovely ones, especially from France, and to be perfectly honest, if anyone is so rude as to look down their nose at your wine of choice, that says far more about them than about you!

JULY

As the summer hurtles on, the holidays approach and the air is filled with the smell of newly cut grass (and petrol fumes from the mowers) and barbecues, take time to appreciate friends.

Old friends, new friends, the friends you see daily or weekly, the ones that logistics mean you only see every few years, the ones you talk to all the time, and the ones you only have time to catch up with occasionally but with whom you are still able to pick up exactly where you left off.

Anyone who can say they have good friends is a lucky person. I know I am hugely lucky to have friends I have known from school, friends I have made through my children – who were considerate enough to pick people with nice parents as their best friends (with hardly any help from me at all … much) – and a few years ago, when I thought I was past the stage of making new friends, some other fabulous, crazy, wonderful people burst into my life quite unexpectedly.

I suppose everyone looks for something different in a friend, but for me, it's someone you can laugh with until you have tears streaming down your legs, but who will also hold you while you cry. It's someone you can confide in about your darkest fears, only to have them raise their eyebrows and point out how ridiculous you are being. It's someone who will genuinely be joyful about your successes, and saddened by your failures and losses, but who will also care enough about you to tell you when you need to pull yourself together, let things go and sort yourself out. It's someone who will encourage you to buy the dress you are worried is too young for you, but who will also stop you buying the dress that makes you look like an over-stuffed sofa.

Don't worry, this isn't going to turn into a lecture about making more time for your friends, or trying to see more of them, because everyone's lives are busy, and *obviously* you would already be doing that if you could, but this month, take time to appreciate Fabulous Friends! Let's think about our Fabulous Friends more, to see if there is anything we could do to be better friends.

July 1st

Let's go back to the beginning with our Fabulous Friends – who is your oldest friend? Have you known each other so long that, to quote my best friend, Hannah, 'We're stuck with each other now, because I'll be over eighty before I find another friend that I've known for longer than half my life.'

....

....

....

....

....

....

....

....

July 2nd

....

....

....

....

....

....

....

....

....

July 3rd Disobedience Day

Apparently this is a day for breaking the small and petty rules, and there are few rules pettier than some of those that come from school. I was delighted when first reading the rules for my children's school to discover that No 1 was 'A breach of common sense is counted as a breach of the rules!' I have shouted this at Peter and Jane many times to no avail, they are utterly lacking in common sense. I thought it was just mine, but other parents have assured me their own precious moppets are equally witless. It makes you feel even more for the teachers, though, who are trying to instil common sense into the sort of children who think headbutting their sibling's foot is a good idea . . .

....

....

....

....

....

July 4th

....

....

....

....

....

....

....

....

....

....

July 5th

....

....

....

....

....

....

....

....

....

....

July 6th

Do your children ever utterly crush your soul by rejecting your treasured classic childhood books out of hand as 'stupid' or 'boring'? And if so, is it OK to think about selling them to a circus (asking for a friend, obviously)?

....

....

....

....

....

....

....

Something to look forward to

OBVIOUSLY, this should involve a friend. Ideally your very bestest friend in the whole wide world, or if that's not possible, your second or third best friend (clearly don't TELL them they are only your second or third best friend, this is still as frowned upon as it was when we were at school).

....

....

....

....

....

....

....

July 7th

....
....
....
....
....
....

July 8th

What are the qualities you admire most in your friends? What is it that makes your friends so Fabulous?

....
....
....
....
....

July 9th

....
....
....
....
....

July 10th Don't Step on a Bee Day

Because bees are important, and we are all banjaxed without them. Go one further than not stepping on a bee, and be a friend to the bees – if you have a garden, build little 'bee hotels' (there are lots of 'how tos' online), and grow lots of bee-friendly plants. Even if you don't have a garden, you can still help the bees. If you come across a bee that is on the ground and seems to be struggling or disorientated, often it is just exhausted or dehydrated, so give it a little bit of sugar or honey dissolved in some water (just make a little puddle of it, close enough for the bee to suck it up) and almost every time it will revive and fly off, and you will get to feel like a bona fide Bee Whisperer!

....

....

....

....

....

....

July 11th

....

....

....

....

....

....

....

July 12th

....

....

....

....

....

....

July 13th

Does anyone else feel a bit judged in the supermarket when all your reusable bags are from a different supermarket and so clearly you are a fickle interloping supermarket tart?

....

....

....

....

....

July 14th

....

....

....

....

....

July 15th

One of the most Fabulous things about really good friends is the ability to laugh with them over almost nothing at all. When was the last time you laughed until you cried with a friend?

....

....

....

....

....

....

....

....

....

....

....

Summer Holidays

Hurrah and huzzah, let the japes and frolics commence! The summer holidays are now upon us all, from the early starters in Scotland and Northern Ireland who finish at the end of June, to England and Wales who have to wait until the end of July to let the fun and games start. Truly, the Famous Five's parents didn't know they were born, turning their offspring loose with nothing more than bicycles or a leaky dinghy and a cove full of wreckers or an island inhabited exclusively by beastly crims to entertain them for the summer. An egg sarnie, a few gooseberries, a dash of ginger ale, and the precious moppets were gone for weeks! Now, alas, we must spend the GDP of Luxembourg on Sports Camps and Activities Weeks and on taking them on holiday so they can complain about substandard Wi-Fi. I bet Julian, Dick and Anne wouldn't have moaned about Wi-Fi, they would have solved The Mystery Of The Limited Bandwidth, which would probably have been due to the dodgy looking chap next door running an internet crime empire. Oh for the Good Old Days of benign child neglect, when criminals really LOOKED like criminals and were easily detected by their Comedy Accents ...

July 16th

....

....

....

....

....

July 17th

There is nothing like the look of fear on a young male cashier's face when your shopping mainly consists of gin, crisps and tampons . . .

....

....

....

....

July 18th

....

....

....

....

....

July 19th

July has a dearth of amusingly pointless Days – only the odd completely pointless Day like 'Eat Peach Ice Cream Day'. Peach is not even an ice cream flavour, why does it get its own day?

July 20th

July 21st

July 22nd

While we're talking about our Fabulous Friends, we mustn't forget the absent friends. Is there anyone you have lost?

....
....
....
....
....
....
....
....

July 23rd

....
....
....
....
....
....
....
....
....

July 24th Tell an Old Joke Day

Because the old ones are the best! What's green and goes up and down?
A gooseberry in a lift!

What's 300m tall and wobbles?
The Trifle Tower!

What do you call a man with a spade on his head?
DOUG!

What do you call a man without a spade on his head?
DOUGLAS!

....
....
....
....
....
....

July 25th

....
....
....
....
....
....

July 26th

....

....

....

....

....

....

July 27th

Things people without dogs will never say: 'FFS! I have TOLD you: we don't eat things we find on the ground!' (Actually, in fairness, toddler parents probably shout that a lot as well.)

....

....

....

....

....

July 28th

....

....

....

....

....

July 29th

Sometimes being a good friend involves more than just being Fabulous, and only focusing on positives. Sometimes, to be a good friend, you have to have a harder conversation, that maybe they don't want to hear. Have you ever had to do this, and would it have been better to say nothing?

....

....

....

....

....

....

....

July 30th

....

....

....

....

....

....

....

....

July 31st

Winning at Life
Moment of the Month

Hopefully this also involved a Fabulous Friend, and
ideally doing something divine, or at least laughing till
the tears ran down your legs ... (anyone else not totally
realise the importance of those pelvic exercises
till it was too late?)

....

....

....

....

....

....

....

....

Tipple of the Month

Mojito

My friend Sam refers to these as 'Pond', because the amount of greenery in them makes him think of a pond. They are summery, refreshing and perfect to share (and not 'pondy' in flavour at all).

1 tsp brown sugar

2–3 sprigs of mint

1 shot of white rum (as ever, the definition of how much is a 'shot' is up to you!)

Fresh lime

Soda water

Ice

Pop the sugar and mint in a glass and crush them together. If you are a sophisticated cocktail person, you will probably have a special implement to do this, the rest of us will let the side down and use the back of a spoon. Add the rum, plenty of ice, and lime and soda to taste. Guzzle with abandon and dance on the tables, while shouting 'I luvs you guys! No, I DOES, I really luvs you!'

AUGUST

Your phone camera roll.

How many photos of your kids/grandkids/dogs/cats/random stuff/ dinners are in there, and how many photos of you are there, with the rest of the group on days out, or holidays or family occasions? Or are you always behind the camera, capturing those ice-creamy smiles, those birthday candles, those happy faces at the end of a long walk – there, but not there?

I know some people just don't like having their photo taken (I am one of them, point a camera at me, and my best attempts at a nice smile turn into a vaguely threatening rictus-style gurning, so I DO sympathise) whether it's because you don't like the way you look, or you feel self-conscious. But get over it – however much you hate photos of yourself, one day you might be glad to have them to look back at and think 'Wasn't I young/thin/thank god my hair isn't like that anymore'.

It's not just for you though. One day, your kids will be looking back through the photos of their childhood, and if you aren't there, then an enormous chunk of their life will be missing. You should be in the photos for your grandchildren too, and your great grandchildren. Remember how much fun it was looking through your granny's old photos and marvelling at how they looked when they were young, at the clothes they wore, and the hairstyles they had? Photos are also useful to demonstrate to small children that you were not in fact born in the Dark Ages, and people didn't go around in corsets and crinolines in your youth (my grandmother never forgave me for asking if people still wore long dresses when she was young, 'you know, Granny, in the Olden Days …') And worst case scenario, if something was to happen to you, your children and your grandchildren will want photos to remember you by, to put on the mantelpiece, to show people and say, 'that was my Granny, she was pretty hot, wasn't she!'

So this month, get Snap Happy and take at least one photo with you in it, or if you are brave, you could ask a respectable-looking passer by to take a photo of you all, though I am always afraid I will pick a master criminal disguised in a twin set and pearls who will promptly leg it with my phone, and then I will have to explain to the police that I wasn't *mugged* so much as I just hailed them myself and insisted on handing over my phone.

Maybe even print some off!

August 1st

What is your favourite photo of you? My husband's favourite Snap Happy moment of me is me standing on a windy beach, looking cold and bedraggled. I loathe it. He says he loves it because I 'look so happy'. I don't, I look cold and bedraggled, and I also like to remind him of how I whined constantly on that trip because I was so cold and bedraggled, so I am baffled as to why he thinks I look 'so happy'. My favourite photo of me is of me standing next to a huge marble bum at a posh party. I'm warm and dry indoors in a posh frock, with a glass of fizz in my hand and an enormous arse beside me in the name of Art . . . what's not to love!

....

....

....

....

....

....

....

August 2nd

....

....

....

....

....

....

....

....

August 3rd White Wine Day

I mean, it just seems rude not to mention it . . .? Why not celebrate this important day by getting someone to take a photo of you with a glass of white wine, then you can importantly announce it is part of your photography project and not just an excuse to drink wine. You are an Artiste. Or something.

....
....
....
....
....

August 4th

....
....
....
....

August 5th

....
....
....
....
....

August 6th

....

....

....

....

....

....

....

....

....

....

August 7th

Have you ever accidentally turned your camera onto selfie mode without realising, so that when you open up your phone, all you see is your mother staring out at you, and you can't work out why?

....

....

....

....

....

....

....

Something to look forward to

(Something other than school going back, that is . . .)

....

....

....

....

....

....

....

August 8th

Have you had any Snap Happy moments yet? Any you'd be happy to share with the world?

....

....

....

....

August 9th

....

....

....

....

August 10th

Why are pockets in women's clothes still such an unusual thing that we are rendered joyous by the discovery of a skirt or dress or even trousers with proper pockets? We need more pockets!!!!!

....

....

....

....

August 11th Middle Child Day

Apparently the poor old middle children are often the most forgotten – lacking the novelty of the oldest kids or the neediness of the younger kids, they are left to get on with it. So if you have a middle child, today would be a good day to take a photo just with them. Or even if you don't, why not get some photos with you and each of your children individually? Though that is often easier said than done – my children used to be adorable, photogenic cherubs, but by the time they started school, they decided they didn't like having their photos taken, so they gurn hideously whenever I point a camera at them, which means most of our family occasions are commemorated by me shouting 'Just SMILE FFS! I need **#happymemories**. OK, great, now can you both smile at once? Yes, and with your eyes open! No, BOTH of you smiling with your eyes open AT THE SAME TIME. IT'S NOT EFFING ROCKET SCIENCE!' So our photos look like the Addams Family Album.

....
....
....
....
....
....

August 12th

....
....
....
....
....
....

August 13th

August 14th

August 15th

Do you have Snap Happy shots of yourself from B.C. (Before Children)? My daughter's main response to such photos is usually 'What did you think you were wearing?'

August 16th

....

....

....

....

....

....

August 17th

....

....

....

....

....

....

August 18th

Ah, the school holidays! Why not play a fun game with your precious moppets? Every time they say 'I'm bored' you do a shot! On second thoughts, it's quite frowned upon to be paralytic by 7.30am, so maybe not . . .

....

....

....

....

....

August 19th Photography Day

You know what you have to do! On you go. SMILE!

....
....
....
....
....

August 20th

....
....
....
....
....

August 21st

....
....
....
....
....
....

August 22nd

Why not go one further than a Snap Happy selfie and have a photo taken of you that takes you out of your comfort zone? I'm not talking about a 'boudoir shot' in your knickers (though go for it, if you like the idea and have posh pants to show off!) but maybe a photo without make-up?

....

....

....

....

August 23rd

....

....

....

....

August 24th

Is there a special filter on the cameras for passport photos so you look as pants as possible? Is it actually a prerequisite? Do you think sometimes when they send photos back saying they aren't up to the required standard, what they mean is 'You look semi-human in this, therefore it does not meet our stringent "look as pants as possible" standards'?

....

....

....

....

August 25th

....

....

....

....

....

August 26th

....

....

....

....

August 27th Just Because Day

This seems rather a jolly idea – you are supposed to do something nice for no reason at all, 'just because'. And if you can't think of anything else to do, you could always ask someone to take a nice photo of you, 'just because'! Which would be much healthier than my default 'just becauses' which always seem to involve biscuits. Or cake. Or wine. Bugger the picture, actually, just find a biscuit-based wine cake to scoff 'just because' . . .

....

....

....

....

August Bank Holiday

There are two options for Bank Holiday weather: either it will tip it down or it will be hotter than Hades. If it is peeing it down, it is traditional to find some wholesome outdoor activity to trudge around until you are so wet you think you might have mildew in your bra, and if it is hot, it is actually the law that you must sit in a traffic jam somewhere, refereeing fights between children who need a wee RIGHT NOW.

August 28th

....

....

....

....

....

....

....

August 29th

So did you go Snap Happy and manage to be in many photos? Any?

....

....

....

....

....

August 30th

....

....

....

....

....

August 31st

Things people without dogs will never say: 'Err, actually I don't have any photos of my real kids on my phone, but do you want to see a photo of Mummy's Most Precious instead?' (This one may also be true of cat people.)

....

....

....

....

....

Winning at Life
Moment of the Month

Did you manage to get a photo of it too? Probably not,
every time I frantically try to capture a **#magicalmoment** it
turns out that my phone is in selfie mode and all that is
captured is me looking deranged and sweaty.

....

....

....

....

....

....

....

....

Tipple of the Month

Aperol Spritz

Not only is this summery and refreshing, it is also a very photogenic drink, and so perfect for this month. I have included two versions; one is a sensible version, while the other is a more turbocharged version, as made by a friend of mine. The turbo spritz is jolly nice, but be warned, it can be very strong.

APEROL SPRITZ

1 shot of Aperol

1 glass of prosecco

Soda water

Ice

Put the ice in a glass, ideally a big wine glass, and add the Aperol and prosecco and top up with a dash of soda water. You can pop in an orange slice to garnish, and as you know, I think a 'brella is never out of place in a cocktail!

TURBO SPRITZ

1 large shot of vodka

1 large shot of Aperol

1 glass of prosecco

Blood orange juice

Ice

Mix it all together, as for the ordinary spritz.
Be prepared to be unable to feel your
face after two glasses.

SEPTEMBER

So, the end of the summer is nigh.

If the kids aren't already back at school they will be any day now, and after a summer of Japes and Frolics (breaking up fights) you are possibly on the verge of a nervous breakdown, just in time to brave shoe shop queues and arguments about why these trousers are FINE, they ARE FINE, well you are buying them anyway because they are the only ones in their size, and no, you're not buying those ones over there, because they are £25 for ONE PAIR and they will only be ruined by half term anyway.

Now that a semblance of 'normal service' (if such a thing even exists) is resuming, take the opportunity to make a bit of time for yourself. I do mean a little bit, I know sometimes there is not even enough time to go for a pee (let alone in peace) but this month, carve out some time to do something that is completely for you alone. As always, this can be big or small, whether you can cash in all your Brownie points and bugger off to a luxury spa for a long weekend, or bribe the kids with the electronic babysitter so you can have one hot cup of tea and five minutes reading showbiz gossip on scurrilous websites in the morning. As long as it's something so you can say 'this moment is All About Me!'

September 1st

What will you do for yourself that is All About Me? Are you aiming for little and often, or one big indulgence?

....

....

....

....

....

....

....

....

September 2nd

....

....

....

....

....

....

....

....

....

Back to School

'Darlings, can you look through your uniform and tell me what you need for going back to school?' Ah ha ha ha ha. Imagine if it was that easy! Obviously, they will need *everything* because anything that the little cherubs haven't managed to lose will have been ripped, stained, trashed and broken, so every year it will be back to square one with the pain, both financial and mental, of kitting them out once more.

Across the country frazzled mothers are in Clarks hissing 'I don't effing care if you don't like them, sweetie, we have tried on every pair of shoes in this shop and these are the only ones that fit you properly and if we don't get out of here in the next THREE MINUTES I am going to beat myself to death with a black lace-up!' This comes before the arguments about the 'right sort of polo shirts', the desperate recollection as to whether they are allowed to wear grey socks or only black ones because M&S only has grey ones left and, worst of all, the hideous foray into the seventh circle of hell that is effing Smiggle. 'A combination of Smile and Giggle' MY ARSE, it is a combination of overpriced, over-scented petroleum by-products, my tears, AND THE LAST TATTERED SHREDS THAT REMAIN OF MY SOUL. I don't like Smiggle. Can you tell?

September 3rd

....

....

....

....

....

September 4th

....

....

....

....

....

September 5th International Day of Charity

If the thought of doing something self-indulgent makes you feel a bit
uncomfortable, you could always offset it and do something good for charity
as well. Even if you can't spare any cash, charities always need people to
donate time.

....

....

....

....

....

....

September 6th

....

....

....

....

....

....

September 7th

....

....

....

....

....

September 8th

Have you done anything that is All About Me yet? If time and money were no object, what would be the most self-indulgent luxury you would treat yourself to?

....

....

....

....

....

September 9th Grandparents' Day

If your family is lucky enough to have fabulous grandparents in your life, who help out with childcare, finances and much more, do something nice for them today, or even just tell them how much they are appreciated!

....

....

....

....

September 10th

Hurrah, they must all be back at school by now! The callouses on your fingers from sewing on eleven billion name tapes are fading (or, if you are a non-sewer, the Sharpie marks from scrawling their name in everything instead, which is really more practical because a name tape could easily be cut out, so, actually, those blurred initials are just you being Extra Vigilant). The brand-new school shoes are scuffed and battered already and despite the careful labelling of every single effing piece of kit and equipment, at least six items have been lost, with only a casual shrug by way of explanation when you shrieked 'HOW? How did you lose it already?' And if that isn't fun enough for you, the LETTERS are starting again. Oh the letters! Or maybe emails. Sometimes texts. Sometimes your school may go for all three, but with no rhyme or reason as to what information is communicated by which method. And, if your bank account is not in a fragile enough state after a summer of 'fun' and all the 'back to school' shopping, not to mention the additional expenses incurred by the little-known rule that any child at home must be fed snacks every fifteen minutes or they are entitled to ring Childline, all these letters require money!

....

....

....

....

September 11th

....

....

....

....

....

....

September 12th

Kids returning to school should herald a lot more time to do constructive things, yet there is still no time. Why is there never enough time? At what point in life do you start having enough time in the day?

....

....

....

....

....

September 13th

....

....

....

....

....

September 14th

....
....
....
....
....
....

September 15th

How is that All About Me time going?

....
....
....
....
....
....

September 16th

....
....
....
....
....
....

September 17th

September 18th

It's that time of year when all of a sudden there are lots of heavily pregnant ladies about and all I can think is 'You must've had a good Christmas/New Year . . .'

September 19th

Something to look forward to

In a month of self-indulgence, this should be something maybe a little bit special? Unfortunately, Tom Hardy claims baby oil gives him a rash . . .

....

....

....

....

....

....

.... !◑#☠*⚡

September 20th

!!!

September 21st *World Gratitude Day*

I know, I know, it's veering dangerously close to self-help w*nk again! But, bear with me! We spend so much time chasing things we haven't got, hankering after things we think we need, longing for stuff that we are *sure* would make our lives better, that sometimes we forget what we *do* have. So, what are you grateful for today? It doesn't have to be deep and meaningful and soulful, it can be as simple as being grateful that you got to go for a wee without anyone banging on the door with an urgent list of demands (aren't we *all* grateful for that?). Or it could be the big stuff.

September 22nd

If you had a magic lamp, but the only wish it could grant you was one extra hour in the day (yes, it's a pretty rubbish magic lamp, I'm sorry), what would you do with it that was All About Me?

....

....

....

....

....

September 23rd

....

....

....

....

September 24th

Why do weekends so often end up being even busier than weekdays? They are meant to be rest days, yet they are frequently spent running round like blue-arsed flies instead, which seems to defeat the point of them!

....

....

....

....

....

September 25th World Dream Day

What was your dream when you were little? When I was seven, my dream was to be called Belinda, as I hated my name. I don't know why 'Belinda' was the name of choice, but I was convinced that if only I was called Belinda, everything else would fall into place. I still think Belinda is a nice name, but safe to say my dreams changed a little over the years. Is your dream a completely impractical, unachievable fanciful notion, like everyone in your house being able to find their own stuff without shouting 'MUUUUUUUMMMMM? Do you know where my XYZ is?' as they insist they HAVE looked, they have looked EVERYWHERE, only for you to find the missing item either *exactly where it is supposed to be,* or *sitting somewhere in plain sight.* If that is your dream, then I'm sorry but you really need to manage your expectations and focus on something achievable like winning the lottery or spending a night with Tom Hardy, Cap'n Poldark and that bottle of baby oil . . .

....

....

....

....

....

....

September 26th

....

....

....

....

....

....

September 27th

Things people without dogs will never say: 'I don't care how scratchy your balls are, stop licking them in public!'

....

....

....

....

....

September 28th

....

....

....

....

September 29th

How did taking some All About Me time feel?

....

....

....

....

....

September 30th

Winning at Life
Moment of the Month

Was your best moment one of your 'moments for you'?
Are you surprised, looking back over the month, about what
your best September moment is?

....

....

....

....

....

....

....

....

Tipple of the Month

Cosmopolitan

While we're on the subject of being selfish and taking time for ourselves, we might as well knock back a few of the favourite cocktails of the most self-centred women who were ever on TV – yes, it's the signature cocktail of the *Sex and the City* girls.

And, of course, Cosmos also have many health benefits, especially for ladies, with all that cranberry juice being excellent for the old waterworks, so we are really practically drinking a spa in a glass, which makes them totally guilt free!

1 shot of vodka (you know the score on measurements by now)

½ shot of Cointreau (if you don't have any Cointreau, any orangey flavoured booze works, and at a pinch, orange juice will do, though it might make the Cosmo a bit cloudy. Don't use orange squash. I cannot possibly reveal how I know this definitely doesn't work)

About ¾ cup of cranberry juice (use a teacup or a small glass if you don't have a measuring cup, it's not an exact science)

Big squeeze of fresh lime juice

Ice

Put everything in a cocktail shaker and give it a good shake. If you don't have a cocktail shaker, a large jam jar will do. Then strain off the ice and pour the cocktail into a martini glass. It really does need to be a martini glass. Sit back and sip, while wishing that tulle skirts and oversized silk corsages were still A Thing.

OCTOBER

The nights are getting darker, the weather is getting colder, the clocks will go back at the end of the month and winter will be here properly.

October is one of those months that really marks the change in the seasons. It (hopefully) starts with crisp, clear days and falling leaves, and ends in long nights and bare black trees. It is also the month when Winter Eating can really begin in earnest. Although I love summer food – fresh salads, herbs, grilled meats (even the wretched barbecues) – there is a reason winter stodge is called 'comfort food', isn't there? No one ever said 'I'm feeling a bit down, I know, a nice salad will cheer me up no end!', did they?

I love food. I love pretty much all food (apart from Hot Tomatoes, you know, those nasty 'grilled' tomatoes that some restaurants inexplicably insist on serving both with breakfasts and with steaks. Just No. Bad and Wrong.). I'm already planning the next meal before I have finished the last mouthful of the current meal. So my heart belongs to winter food – the soups and stews and pies and cakes and root vegetables (no nasty fruits masquerading as vegetables there, ha!) and carbs. So this month, think about some of your favourite foods and recipes. Write them down for your children, or if you are feeling very brave, you could even cook them with your kids. Ask family members for that recipe you have always meant to get from them. Let the Deliciousness of the Winter Eating commence!

October 1st

What is your best memory of food from your childhood? Can you cook any of the dishes you remember from when you were a child? Are they as full of Deliciousness as they were when you were a kid?

....

....

....

....

....

....

October 2nd

....

....

....

....

....

October 3rd

....

....

....

....

....

Something to look forward to

Something involving large amounts of Deliciousness, perhaps? Maybe whipped cream ... doesn't even need to be on a pudding. It's best on a pudding though. Or hot chocolate. Otherwise it's just messy and there is a lingering smell of cheese on the sheets. So I'm told, anyway.

....

....

....

....

....

....

....

October 4th

....
....
....
....
....

October 5th National Cake Week

A whole week, just for cake! The person who manages to invent a diet that
involves eating only cake while sitting on your arse, and still losing weight, will
be a very rich person indeed. I have done extensive research into this, but so
far have only managed to expand my arse, not shrink it, so I think I need
to do a lot more research . . .

....
....
....
....
....

October 6th

....
....
....
....
....

October 7th

....

....

....

....

....

....

October 8th

What is your very favourite food? Is it a proper meal, or is it something simple like Marmite on toast? What gives it the Deliciousness factor for you?

....

....

....

....

....

October 9th

....

....

....

....

....

October 10th

Are you a 'Oh my child eats *anything*' Mummy, or are you a 'Googling symptoms of scurvy over dinner in a desperate effort to persuade them to eat a pea' Mummy? Or did you have one child that ate everything, making you smugger than a smug thing, and another child who crushed your dreams of being the next Annabel Karmel by rejecting anything that wasn't beige with all nutrition processed out of it? What was your top trick (not tip) to get them to eat something that would stave off the gruesome Victorian diseases for another day? Or did you just bang your head against a brick wall while sobbing 'But yesterday that was your FAVOURITE, you little *&^*&^&%*, PLEASE JUST EFFING EAT IT! WHAT DO YOU WANT FROM ME? DO YOU WANT BLOOD?'

....

....

....

....

....

....

October 11th

....

....

....

....

....

....

....

October 12th World Egg Day

Yep, it's a thing apparently. What do you eat with your eggs? (Toast. Toast is the only answer to this.)

....

....

....

....

October 13th

....

....

....

....

October 14th

I have realised the world is divided into three sorts of people: those who wipe down worktops PROPERLY after use, those who don't even bother, and those who make a half-hearted attempt to drag a sodden sponge through the mess, leaving a sort of crumb gruel in their wake. Which are you (please say the first, or I don't think we can be friends)?

....

....

....

....

October 15th

After the entries for cake and eggs, I realised I had great difficulty in writing apparently simple words because after too many years spent with small children, I appear to be incapable of using such words and always default to 'eggies' and 'cakey' instead. TBH, I'm not 100% sure 'Deliciousness' is actually a word either ...

....

....

....

....

....

October 16th

....

....

....

....

October 17th

....

....

....

....

October 18th

October 19th International Gin and Tonic Day

Everything else has a day, so *obviously* gin has to have one too! Are you one of those people who LOVES gin but spends the next day in a sobbing heap with The Fear, weeping over unlikely Worst Case Scenarios and scouring the internet for solutions, while insisting that there is NOTHING WRONG WITH YOU and it WASN'T THE GIN, you are just VERY WORRIED about what will happen when the dog dies, even though that is not likely to happen for another ten years, but you just want to BE PREPARED?

October 20th

I try very hard to be middle-class, but find myself constantly thwarted by **#parentingfails** like discovering the children have been eating out of date houmous. For a week.

....

....

....

....

....

October 21st

....

....

....

....

....

October 22nd

Is there any particular dish or cuisine you've always wanted to make? Do you think it will be as oozing with Deliciousness when you make it yourself?

....

....

....

....

....

October 23rd

October 24th

October 25th World Pasta Day

Celebrate World Pasta Day by making a Nice, Simple Lasagne! You know, that quick and easy dish that in no way uses EVERY POT IN THE KITCHEN AND TAKES ELEVENTY BILLION HOURS TO COOK AND NO ONE APPRECIATES BECAUSE THEY THINK IT IS 'JUST PASTA'? Alternatively, buy a frozen one. And insert it in orifice of choice of the next person who remarks that lasagne is a nice easy dinner.

Clocks Go Back

FFS! They've done it again! 'Oh, but you get an extra hour's sleep!' some people will smugly tell you. Yes. Yes, you do. Assuming you don't have small children who give not one single f*ck that the clocks have changed and so now will wake you up at 4am, which is just salt in the wounds of your sleep deprivation.

October 26th

October 27th

October 28th

Things people without dogs will never say: 'You're not having cheese, it gives you Cheesy Bum' (well, this might apply to some partners too).

....

....

....

....

....

....

....

....

October 29th

....

....

....

....

....

....

....

....

....

October 30th

What was your worst culinary disaster? Do you have any top tips you would pass on to your children (even if it is just 'don't do it, get a takeaway')?

....

....

....

....

....

....

....

....

....

....

....

October 31st Halloween

Ah, Halloween. The ancient festival of All Hallow's Eve, now celebrated with synthetic supermarket costumes and Haribos. Brace yourself for your precious moppet deciding approximately three minutes before you leave the house that either their costume is 'rubbish' or that they no longer want to be Elsa, they want to be a cat/witch/ghost/vampire. (Top tip, keep a supply of old sheets and black clothing to hand and it is amazing the last-minute Halloween costumes you can cobble together – I once made a vampire costume out of an old school shirt, a black bin bag (cloak) and an antiquated pair of my white lace knickers (I cut the gusset out – for the costume, you understand, at all other times I am firmly in favour of a stout gusset) as a 'jabot', threw red food colouring liberally over the lot, denied that was an old pair of knickers and we were good to go! Bats and cats and ghosts and witches have been similarly supplied at short notice, which is part of the reason why I bloody hate Halloween.

Winning at Life
Moment of the Month

Hopefully a divinely calorific moment. Or perhaps a
#smugmummy moment when a moppet said something too
blissfully middle class for words like, 'Please can we get extra
broccoli today, Mummy?' and people HEARD and you beamed
merrily and said 'Of COURSE, poppet!' over the second
half of their sentence which was, 'because the guinea
pigs like it. I wouldn't touch it if you paid me!'

....

....

....

....

....

....

....

....

Tipple of the Month

Manhattan

This is nothing more than shameless hedonism, as Manhattans are quite my favourite cocktail, so I end up drinking a lot of them. They are jolly nice though, and need lots of cherries, which pleases me, as I don't think a cocktail is really a cocktail without a cherry. And ideally a 'brella.

1 shot of rye whiskey (you can use bourbon too, but a) rye whiskey is nicer, and b) I'm not allowed bourbon, because if I drink bourbon I could start a fight in an empty room, which is unfortunate)

2 shots of red vermouth – Martini Rosso is good

Maraschino cherries! All the cherries! And a little bit of the cherry juice from the jar

Ice

Put the ice, booze and a dash of the cherry jar liquid in a cocktail shaker. If you haven't got a cocktail shaker, just go and buy one – you can get them for about a fiver! Or use a jam jar again, if you must. Shake well, and pour into a martini glass, straining off the ice. Add as many cherries as you wish – personally I think a minimum of three is about right. Sip happily. Eat the cherries. Demand another Manhattan. Realise you are drinking neat booze, but decide it doesn't matter because you feel very happy. Tell complete strangers you love them. No, you really, *really* love them.

NOVEMBER

This month, as the temptation to just start hibernating and not come out again till spring starts to creep in, and we batten down the hatches against the cold and the dark, and think that even if actual hibernating isn't an option, it would be nice to just huddle on the sofa under a blanket for the next few months, this is a good time to focus on Our Family.

So whether your family is big or small, whether you can trace your family history back to William the Conqueror, or whether you're not sure of the family tree more than a generation back, this month, think about what makes your family special. Because every family is different and unique, whether you have been married for thirty years with six kids and your parents and in-laws and siblings nearby, or whether you're a single parent to one child with no other family around you, whether your family is biological or adopted, whether you couldn't live without them or they drive you mad, they are *your* family, and that makes them pretty damn special.

November 1st

Where does Your Family come from? Have you ever tried to trace your family tree, and find out more about your history?

....

....

....

....

November 2nd

....

....

....

....

November 3rd Cliché Day

There are so many clichés about families, aren't there? That sisters are supposed to confide in each other and be best friends, that brothers always have each other's backs, that mums are nurturing and love baking, that dads are good at DIY, to name just a few.

....

....

....

....

November 4th

November 5th Bonfire Night

Ah, the crackle of the bonfire, the wide-eyed wonder of childish faces, lit in the glow of the fireworks, the smell of sausages and baked potatoes. The shouts of 'BE CAREFUL WITH THAT SPARKLER, IT IS FIRE, GET IT AWAY FROM YOUR SISTER, ARE YOU TRYING TO SET HER ALIGHT?' The wails of small children with burnt tongues, who were TOLD the sausages were hot and that they needed to wait for them to cool down. The realisation that magical nights like this were probably why hip flasks were invented. And sloe gin.

November 6th

Have you ever considered just running away from them all? Your beloved Family? Just getting in the car and driving off and keeping driving, away from the lost socks and the packed lunches and the never-bloody-ending snacks and the laundry and the unwiped counter tops and the permission slips and the lost PE kits and the fights and the mud immediately walked over the clean floor and shouting about teeth and shoes and shoes and teeth and bloody shoes and effing teeth and just wash your face because I said so and the wittering and the sudden need to bang on the door when you're having a wee, and just running away, to a desert island. A *deserted* desert island. A totally deserted desert island, with no Man Friday to appear and ask if you've seen his coconut, because no, of course he has looked for it, and he can't find it anywhere.

....

....

....

....

....

....

November 7th

....

....

....

....

....

....

November 8th

Do you have anyone you consider 'family' who you are not actually related to, but have known so long and are so close to that they are family to all intents and purposes?

....

....

....

....

....

November 9th

....

....

....

....

....

November 10th

There are few examples of shining maternal instinct so true, so deep, as when your child bursts into the sitting room screaming they are going to be sick and you respond 'WELL, GET IN THE BATHROOM NOW!'

....

....

....

....

....

November 11th Armistice Day

Did any of your family fight in the wars of the last hundred years? How do you remember them?

....

....

....

....

....

November 12th

....

....

....

....

....

November 13th

....

....

....

....

....

Something to look forward to

Don't worry, this doesn't have to involve family if you don't want it to! It's OK to want to escape from your family sometimes. Or most of the time. I honestly think that's why cupboards under the stairs were invented . . .

....

....

....

....

....

....

....

November 14th

....
....
....
....

November 15th

Who makes up your immediate Family? Is this the family you always imagined having?

....
....
....
....

November 16th International Day for Tolerance

Families require a lot of tolerance – all those people who know exactly what buttons to push to annoy you, all those irritating habits you are forced to live with, that *thing* they do – *why* do they do that? – that you *know* they're going to do, even before they do it!

....
....
....
....

November 17th

....

....

....

....

....

November 18th

....

....

....

....

....

November 19th

A really useful tip for using up leftover egg whites is to pop them in the fridge for a week and forget about them before throwing them in the bin!

....

....

....

....

November 20th

....
....
....
....
....

November 21st

....
....
....
....
....

November 22nd

Do you have any strange family traditions? Even if you hate them, and grumble about them, do you think you would miss them if you didn't do them?

....
....
....
....

November 23rd Day of Listening

If you are totally honest, do you always listen to what your family are saying? To your precious moppets' chatter about Pokémon and YouTube, to your partner's views on sheds, to your mother's witterings about what Auntie Susan said yesterday? Or do you just sort of tune them out and make vague noises to imply you are definitely paying attention? On the official Day of Listening, why not actually listen closely to what they are all saying, if only to reassure yourself that they are really just babbling on about inanities and you're not missing out on anything interesting. Did it make any difference or could you just have stayed in your happy place, imagining, well whatever it is you imagine in your happy place?

....

....

....

....

....

....

....

November 24th

....

....

....

....

....

....

....

November 25th

What was the most unexpected thing you discovered about having a family of your own? Apart of course from the fact that you now pretty much live in your car, are resigned to the fact that for the rest of your life you will shout 'Cow! Horsey! Sheepy!' every time you pass a field, attempt to persuade co-workers to play 'Yellow Car' and frighten them with your competitiveness if you have a work trip anywhere, and have been known to bark 'SHOELACES! Do you want to break your neck?' at startled strangers in public places, along with a barely controlled desire to spit on a tissue and scrub their faces every time you see someone with something stuck to their cheek or chin . . .

....

....

....

....

....

....

November 26th

....

....

....

....

....

....

....

November 27th

Things people without dogs will never say: 'I don't love the dog MORE than you, I just love him DIFFERENTLY ...'

....

....

....

....

....

November 28th

....

....

....

....

....

November 29th

What are your hopes and dreams for your Family in the future?

....

....

....

....

....

November 30th St Andrew's Day

The Patron Saint of Scotland. The only one of the UK's national saints who was also one of the Apostles. Sadly, very little else is known about him apart from that, but St Andrew's Day is usually celebrated in Scotland by small children informing their mothers at 8.57am that they need to wear something tartan to school that day. Even though St Andrew never actually wore tartan.

....

....

....

....

....

....

....

....

....

Winning at Life
Moment of the Month

Perhaps it was an unexpectedly lovely moment when your moppets decided to stop fighting and behaving like feral weasel cats and be nice for a second, and more like Other People's Children. Yes, I know, I'm an incurable optimist, but the alternative of accepting that the feral weasel cats are as good as it gets is too depressing.

....

....

....

....

....

....

....

....

Tipple of the Month

Rioja

It's winter, it's dark, who can be arsed getting out from under their blanket to faff around making cocktails? Have a nice hearty glass of Rioja instead! Rioja is characterised by interesting top notes of wondering why it isn't bedtime yet and guilt over electronic babysitters. Best paired with All The Carbs that you are eating to keep out the cold because you don't have to worry about Christmas parties or bikini bodies yet.

DECEMBER

It's finally here! It's Christmas time!

You either love Christmas or you hate it. I love Christmas, but I do feel it needs to be restricted only to December – I get enraged by the smuggety smug smug people who like to tell you how many Fridays are left till Christmas . . . in JUNE, or the people who announce they've finished their Christmas shopping in AUGUST, or, the smuggest of all, the people who gleefully inform you on the 3rd January that they have already bought all their Christmas presents for the next Christmas in the sales (I did try doing this once, I carefully put everything in a Safe Place, and then come the next Christmas I couldn't find anything).

So December is for Christmas, and fairy lights and mince pies and roaring fires and carols and apple-cheeked moppets tumbling around in tasteful pyjamas, and presents and eggnog (does anyone actually drink eggnog? Does anyone even know what eggnog is? It sounds festive, but also disgusting) and festive joy and cheer. At least, that is what it is supposed to be like, and hopefully that *is* what it is like for our children, but the actual reality always seems to be a lot of stress and not enough time, and rushing around like a headless chicken for a month.

So, whether you are filled with Festive Cheer or have more Grinch-like feelings about Christmas, or whether like me you begin the month filled with excitement but somewhere along the way, when it's 3am and you have sellotape in your hair and you can't find the scissors you had *just* a minute ago and people keep wittering at you about effing *stuffing* and you are seriously considering throwing the wretched turkey out the window and there is *glitter* EVERYWHERE and you haven't posted the Christmas cards, and Simon wants to know if you've heard from his sister Louisa and what you bought for her hundred kids, then the magic seems to lose a little of its shine, and by the end of the month, you are just completely over Christmas. So you can record your feelings about the whole shebang here if you hate Christmas, and vent about tinsel and consumerism and excess. Or if the magic is real for you, just put it all down to remind yourself of the fun through the rest of the year.

December 1st

*What are the best things about Christmas, and what are the worst? Even the grinchiest Grinch must be able to find **something** to like about Christmas, and even the most dedicated Elf must have **some** festive dislikes amidst the Festive Cheer!*

....

....

....

....

December 2nd

....

....

....

....

December 3rd Make a Gift Day

You probably don't have time for this, but it could occupy small children for an hour or two. Of course, it will probably take you longer to start them off, and then clear up the mess, which will inevitably involve glitter, than they actually spend on making gifts, but it might win some Brownie points with grandparents.

....

....

....

....

December 4th

December 5th

December 6th

Everybody else in the world: Are you all ready for Christmas?
Me: No, there's still weeks to go, there's loads of time!
Also me: FML, Christmas is mere weeks away! PANIC! PANIC! WTF am
   I going to do????

A FESTIVE something
to look forward to

So many lovely things to look forward to in December! So few turn out as you hoped they would! So give yourself an actual treat as well, in between all the **#makingmemories** and **#magicaltimes** that you are creating for everyone else, who are probably very unreasonably refusing to be suitably impressed by the **#magicalf*ckingwonderland** you are trying to make for them.

....

....

....

....

....

....

....

December 7th

....

....

....

....

....

....

December 8th

Do you have any special Christmas traditions in your family to facilitate the Festive Cheer?

....

....

....

....

....

December 9th

....

....

....

....

....

....

December 10th

Whatever day you choose to put up your tree, is it a day of festive cheer, with a bit of emotion as you pile every decoration your precious moppets have ever made onto the tree while sobbing, 'Remember when you made this when you were five, sweetie?' and they mumble something in disgust and embarrassment? Or does everyone pitch in while you twitch and make 'helpful' suggestions like, 'Just a bit to the right, darling!' while thinking 'WHAT IS WRONG WITH THEM? Why can't they see they are putting everything in one place, BALANCE, it needs BALANCE!' and long for them to go to bed so you can do it properly? Or do you just go full-on Tree Nazi and announce it is YOUR TREE and you are doing it properly because IT IS MAGICAL, while snarling at anyone who tries to touch your baubles (ooh err).

....

....

....

....

....

....

December 11th

....

....

....

....

....

....

....

December 12th Gingerbread House Day

Gingerbread houses seem like a very good idea, but always end in someone crying (usually me) and unfeasible amounts of icing smeared on every surface and hyperactive children who have eaten all the sweets they were supposed to use to decorate the house. And then the whole thing has gone soggy by the next day. And yet, each year, we do it again.

....

....

....

....

December 13th

....

....

....

....

December 14th

Lo, is there any other season that causes women to run amok panic buying potatoes and tinfoil and goose fat and All The Gin?

....

....

....

....

December 15th

What is your favourite Christmas food that you don't get the rest of the year? Do you stuff yourself on it, in the name of Festive Cheer?

....

....

....

....

....

December 16th

....

....

....

....

December 17th

#TopChristmasDietTip: bags of Lindt balls make a very similar rustling noise to dog treats, so if you have a furry friend in the house, every time you try to sneak yourself a little something, you will be greeted by a hopeful yet reproachful little face, making you feel guilty and greedy in equal parts!

....

....

....

....

....

School Christmas Party/Christmas Concert

As well as festive joy and cheer, December also brings with it the joy of the Christmas Concerts and Christmas Parties. For the concert, you will either be informed at no notice whatsoever that they need a space ghost costume (so festive) or you will actually receive the note about the costume, requesting you send in yellow leggings with lime-green polka dots and an orange polo neck with purple piping, but exhorting you to make sure these are all 'old clothes' as they will be cut up, even though these are not things that anyone actually just has lurking in their wardrobe, except possibly CBeebies presenters. Then you will get to sit through the concert itself, which is probably something 'modern', trying to spot your child, while thinking judgemental thoughts about how, yes, every child should have a part, but what is wrong with a plethora of shepherds, why on EARTH is there a Christmas giraffe in the stable in Bethlehem? If you are very lucky, though, the tinies will still do a proper Nativity, and you can have a lovely little festive blub.

The Christmas Party is usually fine, as long as you can get your name down quick to provide the crisps and not get stuck peeling and chopping the carrot sticks for thirty kids who are never even going to look at them, and you remember to send them in with their party clothes (unless you are the sort of nice mummy who lets them come home at lunchtime and get changed). Just remember to brace yourself at hometime for your precious moppets being smacked off their tits on weak orange squash and overexcitement!

December 18th

....

....

....

....

December 19th

What was the best present you ever gave someone? Was it a big gift that you knew they would love, or was it something small that you were surprised at how thrilled they were with it? Does giving gifts fill you with Festive Cheer, or do you prefer receiving presents?

....

....

....

....

....

....

December 20th

....

....

....

....

December 21st

....

....

....

....

....

December 22nd

I usually have my Christmas Meltdown around now (I used to have it on Christmas Eve, but I found it easier to get it out of the way earlier). Are you stressed and irritable and feeling like there is just too much to do and nobody is helping, and your Festive Cheer is rapidly evaporating, or are you floating from Christmas party to Christmas party in a sparkly frock on a cloud of champagne? (So jealous . . .)

....

....

....

....

....

December 23rd

....

....

....

....

....

December 24th Christmas Eve

Do your children still believe in Santa? What do you do for Santa? Mince pie and a glass of milk, or something more elaborate? (Apparently our Santa is very fond of a large single malt, rather than a glass of milk.)

December 25th Christmas Day

Merry Christmas! Hopefully the dinner is in the oven, the children are playing happily with their presents, you received tasteful and thoughtful gifts yourself and there is peace on earth and goodwill to all men. Or, more likely, you are sweaty and angry and have spent the morning trying to find some obscurely sized batteries for a piece of noisy tat some sadistic relative gave them, while accidently stabbing yourself in the hand trying to wrench off the completely OTT packaging that toys now come screwed into, dinner is two hours behind schedule, Granny is off her tits on Bristol Cream, one child is crying because the dog has eaten their new ZhuZhu hamster and although deep down you are not sorry about the effing hamster's demise, you are wondering if you should call the vet, another child has abandoned all their expensive presents in favour of playing with a cardboard box, your beloved has decided now would be a good time to bugger off and sort out their sock drawer, and you are giving serious consideration to locking yourself in the kitchen with a bottle of gin and sobbing as you scroll through social media because everyone else IN THE WHOLE WORLD EVER is having a Perfect Christmas, except for you. They're not though. Their Christmas is probably going much like yours. So have a sharpener, whack a filter on a photo to hide the blood/tear stains, slap a **#sofestivelyblessed** caption on it, and take a deep breath. Oh, and hide the sherry from Granny, she can be a bit borderline racist after a few. And one day you'll only remember the good bits.

....

....

....

....

....

....

....

....

December 26th Boxing Day

I know, I know, it's called Boxing Day because it was the day that the rich people boxed up food and gifts for those less fortunate than themselves, but it might equally well be called Boxing Day because it is also the day that your darling children spend pounding each other on a massive comedown from the Christmas excitement because they are already bored with their presents, and you consider punching yourself in the face in preference to eating any more turkey!

....
....
....
....

December 27th

....
....
....
....

December 28th

Things people without dogs will never say: 'Can I get a tetanus shot please, I tried to dress Mummy's Most Precious up as an elf and offended his dignity!'

....
....
....
....
....

December 29th

....

....

....

....

....

December 30th

....

....

....

....

....

December 31st New Year's Eve

Well, that's another year almost finished! Are you celebrating tonight, or having a quiet evening at home? How was the past year for you? What is your one wish for next year?

....

....

....

....

....

....

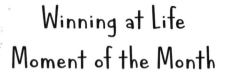

Winning at Life
Moment of the Month

....

....

....

....

....

....

....

....

....

Winning at Life
Moment of the Year

Can you pick one stand out moment from this year, that if you could bottle it and keep it, might even be better than gin?

....

....

....

....

....

....

....

....

Tipple of the Month

Bloody Mary

I did look up what was in Eggnog, and I was underwhelmed, and also, it seems a massive faff to make. So, as the festive season often leaves some of us feeling a little . . . jaded . . . and in honour of the only time of the year when it is not only socially acceptable to start drinking in the morning, but actually encouraged, it had to be the best hangover cure in the world. Everybody has their own ideas about how to make the perfect Bloody Mary, so this is just my version. There are many other things you can add, too – some people like to put in horseradish, which frankly makes it look like sick (not what you want with a hangover) and a stick of celery is a very popular garnish, but I am not keen, as a) I think celery is the work of the devil, and b) the celery stick tends to poke you in the eye when you try to take a drink, which is also not conducive to easing a hangover.

252

1 shot of vodka (don't make this too large a shot, as if you are hungover, you will just top yourself up and be hammered again, and even if you're not hungover, having to be put to bed before lunchtime is never a good look)

Tomato juice

Good squeeze of lemon juice

Black pepper

Tabasco sauce

Celery salt (surprisingly nice, even though it is contaminated with the devil's vegetable – it's not essential if you don't have any, though)

Ice

Put the ice, vodka, tomato and lemon juice in a tall glass, and add black pepper and Tabasco to taste, depending on how spicy you want it. Give it a good stir – if you are using a celery stick to garnish, you can stir it with this. Take a gulp. Wait for the pain to pass and the will to live to return.

HarperCollins*Publishers*
1 London Bridge Street
London SE1 9GF

www.harpercollins.co.uk

First published by HarperCollins*Publishers* 2018

2

A catalogue record of this book is
available from the British Library

ISBN 978-0-00-831426-2

Printed and bound at GPS Group

MIX
Paper from
responsible sources
FSC™ C007454

This book is produced from independently certified FSC™ paper
to ensure responsible forest management.

For more information visit: www.harpercollins.co.uk/green

Find out why Mummy's precious moppets
have driven her to drink

WHY MUMMY DRINKS

OUT NOW!

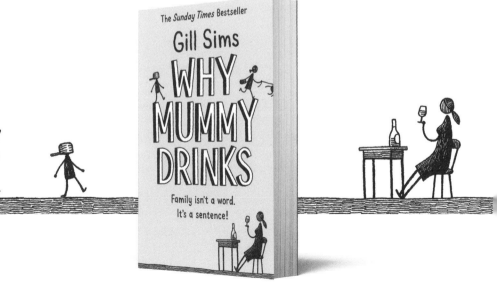

The hilarious *Sunday Times* bestselling debut